'A book th... ... aspiring s...
close to her heart if she wa...
swash. A tale with a big...
Frank Cottr...

'Janina is the most passionate history lover I know,
and it shows. This is a captivating story brimming
with authentic details, and written with sparkling
prose. It made me wish I were a Viking.'
Greg Jenner

'I enjoyed the book very much. The characters were
engaging and the story full of life and movement. It's
not a period, or a place, that I know very much about,
so I was pleased to find things to learn as well as enjoy.'
Philip Pullman

'My daughter would not let me put this down.
We finished it in one sitting!'
Dan Snow

'Vikings! Sassy girl heroes! Runes and wolves!
What's not to like?'
David Aaronovitch

'The historical novel arrives for a new generation—
Alva is a riddle-solving, crime-busting hero from the
Viking ...   ...anced.'

'A gripping mystery that brings the Viking world to vivid life, with a brave and original heroine who'll inspire young readers (and old!) with a passion for historical adventure.'
S.J.Parris

'This is the perfect adventure, and the best new literary heroine I wish I'd met as a child. Bring on the next Alva adventure. She's awoken my shield maiden! This book will transport you to a land of Viking legends and you won't want to put it down!'
Anita Rani

'Janina Ramirez has the mind of a history lover, and the heart of a fun-loving adventurer. She has written a classic detective story in which the clues are buried in runic writing and the carvings on a mysterious casket. The book is set in the 'so-called' Dark Ages but brings them to life in an enthralling and contemporary way.'
Tony Robinson

'Brilliant, warm, and exciting!'
Jenny Colgan

'I thought it was fantastic and EXACTLY the kind of book I want my child to read: educational, great role models, and very entertaining!'
Xand van Tulleken

'This is one of those rare books you can read to a child as they fall asleep and which you'll then stay up the whole night reading yourself. Simply and beautifully written it is an utterly compelling book packed with historical detail, deep characters, and a quest that drives you together with Alva and her wolf across the mountains and into the forests of Viking Scandinavia.'
Chris van Tulleken

'A ferocious heroine as strong as steel—and a mystery worthy of her skills. You'll love it.'
Lucy Worsley

'A brilliant, burning tale all set to fire up the fabulous shield maidens and masters of the future and across the world.'
Bettany Hughes

'Steeped in Viking lore and enriched with all the vibrant colour of Norse mythology, this is a tale to be enjoyed by all, young or old . . .
I had the enormous pleasure of reading this saga with my own little shield maiden, my daughter, Freyja, who sat wide-eyed throughout. We loved the adventure as a Viking loves mead!
More, please!'
Giles Kristian

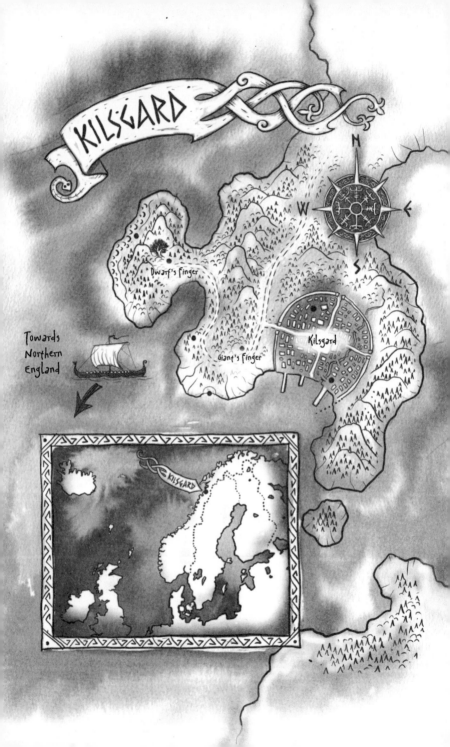

KILSGARD

N
W   E
S

Dwarf's Finger

Towards
Northern
England

Giant's Finger

Kilsgard

KILSGARD

Meet the characters

Alva

Fenrir

Hraf

Uncle Magnus

Brianna

Sigrunn

This is dedicated to the young minds
that feed mine every minute of every day,
Kuba and Kama. Our journey together
will be full of adventures.

OXFORD
UNIVERSITY PRESS

Great Clarendon Street, Oxford OX2 6DP

Oxford University Press is a department of the University of Oxford.
It furthers the University's objective of excellence in research, scholarship,
and education by publishing worldwide. Oxford is a registered trade mark of
Oxford University Press in the UK and in certain other countries

British Library Cataloguing in Publication Data
Data available

ISBN: 978-0-19-276633-5

1 3 5 7 9 10 8 6 4 2

Printed in Great Britain

Paper used in the production of this book is a natural,
recyclable product made from wood grown in sustainable forests.
The manufacturing process conforms to the environmental
regulations of the country of origin.

Use the Viking alphabet at the back of this book to unlock the hidden
meaning behind the rune shown at the start of each chapter.

JANINA RAMIREZ

RIDDLE OF THE RUNES

A VIKING MYSTERY

ILLUSTRATED BY DAVID WYATT

OXFORD
UNIVERSITY PRESS

In search of Great Treasure

Alva was running. Running so fast the wind whistled in her ears and the braids in her bright red hair lashed against her face. She was like a wolf. She was stealthy. She was strong. The tallest mountain in Kilsgard, Giant's Finger, rose ahead through the sunken mist. To her left, sheer cliffs reached out over the angry, black waters of the river howling against the rocks below. She was faster than the water. She was faster than the wind. But one wrong step and Alva would become water and wind. She must be sure on her feet. She must not fall.

Sharp branches cut the skin on her bare legs as she smashed the forest floor beneath her shoes. No time for pain. Now she needed the wits of a shield maiden. She must see everything, and be prepared for anything. Her pet wolf, Fenrir, kept dipping in and out of view ahead of her, his paws silent on the leaves, and his silver fur flashing in and out of the moonlight. He had the scent. He was taking her where she needed to go.

But as her leather soles leapt over rock and branch, suddenly the forest reached out a knotted hand. Alva's foot caught against a root and time slowed. Tumbling, the edge of the cliff filled her vision. The roar of the river grew deafening, as her heart bashed hard against her ribcage. She could see the black jaws of the river's mouth reaching towards her, and Giant's Finger reared up, dark, over her head as she fell.

Bang. Bang. Bang.

Alva sat bolt upright on her straw mattress. She wasn't in the water. She was home. A film of sweat wrapped around her body like a shroud. The fire still gave off an orange glow and she saw her family stirring, disturbed by the loud thud on the door.

'Thor's bones!' Her Uncle Magnus was shouting now. Her little brother, Ivan, gave a howl at having been roused from his sleep, and her mother, Brianna, pulled the grizzling child into an embrace to comfort him. 'In the name of all the gods, what do you want?' Magnus bellowed, swinging his woollen cloak over his bare shoulders. In the half-light Alva could see the scars of old battles etched on his back, but she looked away quickly and squeezed up next to her mother, who wrapped her long, pale arms around her.

'Magnus!' A deep voice called through the thick wooden door. 'There's an epic saga playing out in the hall right now! Jarl Erik says we need you.'

'What time is it?' Magnus replied, swinging open the door to reveal two karls armed with swords. 'And why have you come to my home with iron in your fists?'

'Forgive us, but there is danger in the air tonight. You will learn more when you get to the hall. We are in the small hours between night and morning.' One of the men poked his bearded young face inside and saw Alva, Brianna, and Ivan huddled together at the far end. 'Our apologies for rousing you all. We just need Magnus, but please, there is nothing to worry about. Go back to sleep.' Alva, still reeling from her dream, bristled at the sight of the armoured men inside the safety of her home. She nuzzled closer to her mother and pulled the covers over her body.

Catching the look of concern on the two men's faces, Magnus went to his boots and began pulling them onto his feet. 'I'll bring the bird. He may be useful.' Lifting his tame raven, Hraf, from his perch by the door, Magnus placed the black bird gently on his shoulder. Hraf ruffled his feathers and let out a sleepy caw. Alva felt a stab of jealously towards the bird. Despite the cold and the darkness, she wished that she could join her uncle and discover what was happening in the great hall.

'It's not time for waking yet,' her uncle said gently towards the back of the hut. 'You three must get some more sleep, because that rascal

Ivan will be up, wailing for his breakfast, before long.' As if seeing her thoughts, he caught Alva's eye before adding, 'All of you need to go back to sleep.' Then, grumbling to the two karls, he slammed the door behind him and Alva heard his voice drifting away down the street.

'Magnus is right,' Brianna said, giving her daughter a squeeze and laying her back down on the mattress. 'We must get some sleep. I need you to run some important errands for me tomorrow. Plus, we will have to keep this one busy.' She gestured at the bundle of red hair that was the top of Ivan's head. Alva's brother had already fallen back to sleep and now Brianna curled herself around him.

Calm fell over the family, and soon Brianna's quiet snores sank into a broken rhythm with Ivan's. But Alva was wide awake. Her nightmare had stayed imprinted on her memory and her heart was still pattering much too fast in her chest. Had she seen her own death? Perhaps the gods were sending her a warning. She lay still, eyes closed, and, in the darkness visualized herself as a raven swooping over Kilsgard— peering into the hall, where she could see her uncle in conversation with the Jarl.

From the expressions on their faces it was clear that the karls brought news of danger and drama. Something serious was happening in Kilsgard and her mind began turning over possible scenarios. Was the town under attack? Had something happened to the Jarl? Had there been an omen from the gods? She knew she shouldn't give in to her desire to know more, but Alva was desperate to hear the speeches in the hall tonight. Her mother would be so angry if she awoke and found her daughter missing. But she had to take that risk. She had to follow Magnus. She had to investigate. After all, that's what she was—an investigator.

As she eased herself up from the mattress, the straw inside crackled and creaked. Alva held her breath, but her mother and brother snored on. Fetching her cloak from a hook, she wrapped it tightly around her and slid on her shoes. She moved silently across the room, carefully avoiding the floorboards she knew would make a sound, and bent down to look under the table. Here, on a thick woollen blanket, her wolf Fenrir lay fast asleep. She pressed her face up close to his muzzle, and whispered, 'Fen.'

His eyelids snapped open, revealing two black

pupils outlined with sea-blue rings. As Fenrir realized it was Alva, he rapidly began to bang his tail on the floor in excitement.

'Shhhhh!' she said, placing her hands on his wagging tail to muffle the sound. 'You're coming with me, silly wolf.' Alva got to her feet and Fenrir followed, padding quietly across the rushes on the floor.

The door made a loud whining noise as she heaved it open. Catching her breath, Alva turned back to see if anyone had noticed. Her brother was staring at her from underneath a curtain of her mother's auburn hair.

'Go back to sleep, Ivan,' she whispered across the room. He held her gaze for a moment, then shut his eyes. With dread flowing through her veins like ice, Alva slid through the door. She found herself in a biting-cold night, and Fenrir gave a small, gruff snort, to show that he too was rather annoyed at being outside.

'Come on, Fen,' she said, setting a quick pace in the direction of the hall. Only a silvery, pale glow from a half-moon lit the edges of the houses, but she knew the way without needing to see. Alva had lived in this town her whole life, and she knew every alley, every person, and everything that happened within the walls of Kilsgard. She made it her business to know. A lost chicken or a broken fence, an argument over payment or a secret message passed between lovers—she saw everything.

Alva's hunger for investigating mysteries had been fed by her uncle. Magnus had travelled the world, growing in knowledge with each of his forty winters. He knew so much about so many things, and could pick apart information like a mouse unfurling a nut. But she knew more than him about one thing—Kilsgard, and all that happened in it. She could go unnoticed, hide behind hedges, and peer through cracks. She knew the people of this town inside out. So really, it was her business to know what was going on in the hall right now. Wasn't it?

This hall, this town, and these people were all Alva had ever known, and to her they were perfect. Kilsgard had its own harbour, which could be filled with up to twenty ships when the men were getting ready to go a-Viking. The huts of the villagers were comfortable and warm, even in the cruel winter months. Their yards—noisy with the calls of chickens, pigs, and sheep—backed on to one another, so Alva could leap over the fences to reach the homes of her friends, and disappear for adventures in the woods. Her insatiable need for adventure would land her in trouble, everyone said so. Everyone said the Fates would not protect her forever.

But the villagers were all asleep now and the only flicker of lights came from the great hall—Meginsalr. This was the home of Jarl Erik. He could trace his ancestry back to the founding fathers, and from there to the god Odin himself. His hearth was the centre of Kilsgard.

Even though it was the dark heart of the night, Meginsalr was vibrating with activity.

Drawing closer, Alva could hear her uncle's voice ringing out across the room. She leant silently against the doorway, pressing her ear to the wood. The sounds from inside were clear and Alva immediately realized all the karls were inside together. That was not good. It meant something that affected the whole town was unfolding in the dark of the night.

'I don't understand what you are telling me, Erik!' Magnus bellowed. 'It is such a strange story. There are too many holes in it, and if I am to investigate any further I need all the information laid out before me. The karls can take to the benches and I will hear from this stranger myself about what has happened tonight. I know the tongue he speaks.' Alva could just make out strange words in a foreign language murmuring nervously beneath the noise of the hall.

'He babbles in a messy manner,' one of the karls answered. 'We can't understand him.'

'He speaks the words of the men across the sea,' explained Magnus. 'The English. On my travels I learnt enough of their words that I can translate and tell you what he says. But you must sit silently as he is frightened and I must work hard to unravel his tale.' Alva could hear benches scraping as men sat down to listen, and her heart quickened. She was going to hear a man speak the language of the English. Magnus spoke again, 'Bring the monk forward.'

A voice rose up, 'What is a monk?'

Magnus responded curtly, 'I said no interruptions! You're in the presence of a monk. This man here is one. Just look at his robe and hair.' Alva cursed the solid wooden door obscuring her view of this fascinating man from overseas. Magnus continued, 'the English worship one god, not many. They do not have seers, they have priests who speak to the people, and another group of holy men and women who lock themselves inside sacred buildings to say prayers all day. These are monks, and this is one of them. Now quiet so we can hear him speak.'

A different voice began, quietly and anxiously, to talk in a version of Alva's own tongue which sounded like it had gone loose at the edges. She listened intently. The language was like the Norse they spoke, but the words were longer, rounder, and softer. As the monk spoke, Magnus relayed his phrases back to the hall.

'The stranger says his name is Edmund, of the monastery of Lindisfarne in the Kingdom of Northumbria, along the coast of the Northern Sea. He has been a monk of that place since he was a young boy of eight winters, which means he has passed fifteen years inside its walls.'

Alva knew tales of the island of Lindisfarne. She had heard them from her father and her uncle. A shiver ran down her spine at the mention of it. One of the karls yelled out from the benches, 'Lindisfarne! That useless little island on the northern coast of the English? I remember our trip there well. The promise of great wealth was hardly fulfilled, and the simpering weak men there would not lift an arm in defence of their lands. He is one of those weaklings—our enemies. Why should we listen to him?'

Magnus replied furiously, 'why do you Norse men know nothing but the sounds of your own voices! Listen, he has come to us from our mountain, and his story is bound up with our town. We should hear more.' Speaking again to the monk, he continued translating. 'He says he has travelled a long, hard journey to Kilsgard in search of "a treasure beyond compare". He and his companion, an English warrior named Wiglaf of Bamburgh, have followed clues etched on a mysterious bone casket, which they "found" while travelling abroad.'

Crouched by Alva's feet, Fenrir gave a loud snuffle. She hushed him gently and continued to press her ear to the cold wood, straining to hear more about this enigmatic box.

'The monk says this casket was covered in symbols which he and his companion struggled to decode, and that the individual they had collected it from was a drunkard from our land. This man of Kilsgard had a loose tongue, and told them the runes would lead to Lindisfarne's lost treasures. It brought them here, but they could go no further, since they could not get the final clues from the casket.'

'This is crazy,' another karl shouted suddenly. 'A mystery casket, "found" abroad yet speaking of treasures here? We know what treasures there are in Kilsgard, since we brought most of them here to the Jarl's hall after we went a-Viking. This is all nonsense. Who is this drunkard from our land, and why would the monk and his companion travel all this way because of some runes?'

'I don't yet know all the answers, Eluf,' Magnus replied, sounding frustrated. Alva steeled herself. She had learnt never to question Magnus part-way through his investigations. 'If you keep interrupting me, we will never get to the heart of the mystery.' He turned again to the monk, and continued with his broken narrative. 'He says he and his companion, Wiglaf, set up camp in a clearing on Giant's Finger, but were attacked in the night while sleeping. The monk watched a figure in a cloak strike his friend over the head, drag him to a horse, and then ride away. Terrified and alone, he has come to the home of his enemy in the hope of saving his friend.

'The monk speaks all of this sincerely.'

Magnus said. Alva shuddered as the twinned voices of her uncle and the monk died down. This tale was fascinating! A secret casket covered with codes that needed deciphering. Travellers across seas searching for hidden treasure. A lone figure attacking men on the mountain and dragging them away. It was the stuff of Alva's dreams and yet it was unfolding right now. Her body thrummed with excitement and fear.

Another voice spoke up. 'But why should we waste our time on this English monk?'

Magnus spoke with anger. 'Can't you see the importance of this? A man is missing on our mountain. He was attacked and dragged away. This means there is a kidnapper, or potentially a murderer, roaming the outskirts of Kilsgard. We have to protect the people, and to do that, we have to unpick the strands of this story.'

'Ha ha!' thought Alva, 'I'm just the person to unravel this mystery. Magnus will definitely need my help tonight!'

Magnus continued speaking behind the wall of oak, 'Jarl Erik, we must treat the monk as a guest of this hall. His people have been attacked by our people, and it took courage to come here in the death of night. You should set up safe quarters for him outside, since he will not want to sleep inside the hall with the men.'

Alva heard the familiar and warm tones of Jarl Erik. 'Magnus, you are the best at leading such investigations. You shall take two of my karls with you to the place the monk said he was attacked, and then you can test the truth of his words.' A slight grumble murmured through the hall. Alva knew the men would not be pleased that Magnus was yet again being shown special favour by the Jarl.

The conversation shifted to discussing where the man should sleep, who should support his claim for hostage rights, and who should travel with Magnus. Stepping away from the doorway, Alva rapidly turned over the monk's story in her mind. She knew she should creep back to bed. Her mother was so tired, because Ivan had a touch of elf-shot and had been screaming in pain for the last few nights. She should do the right thing and be ready to help at daybreak. But then Alva saw the monk's travelling cloak lying by the entrance, and the decision crystallized in her mind. The mystery was too much temptation for her.

She was going to help her uncle unravel the

monk's story. Magnus was taking too long, discussing all the details and worrying over the visitor. She had to move fast, as clues could be lost if they delayed. Hadn't he told her that himself? Grasping the monk's cloak, she rubbed its scent under Fenrir's muzzle. 'Follow,' she said, and the silver wolf set off at once, leading her deep into the forest.

The main gates of the town were unguarded, because all the karls had rushed to the hall when the stranger arrived. There was a long pathway which ran along the river. It branched off after a few hundred paces, with one road leading out to the north, and a second winding up towards Giant's Finger.

The mountain looked silent and brooding in the moonlight. It had many moods and Alva knew them all. She spent more time exploring its rocks and crevices than was normal for a girl of her age. In her twelve winters, she had been drawn back to the mountain time and again, in search of evidence for the tales her people told of the Great Battle, when giants and dwarves carved out the landscape.

She wanted to believe these myths, but her keen eyes found no sign of the tens of thousands of bodies that were supposed to lie at the root of the mountain. Alva always believed what her eyes saw over what her ears heard. But recently she had been drawn to the mountain for another reason—for the connection it held with her father. They had walked here together before he left, and here she could feel a little closer to him. She could also escape the tense atmosphere of the family home.

Alva carried on running up the steep slopes of Giant's Finger, as the main route twisted away from the high incline. Her mind wasn't on where she was going, after all she had climbed these paths hundreds of times before. Instead she thought about her uncle and the tensions that had been increasing within their once close little family. When her father was in Kilsgard everyone was happy. He would take her on adventures. Magnus would occupy her with stories from his travels and insights into the many mysteries he'd solved. Her mother would gently chide both men for the way they treated Alva like their equal. But since Father had left the mood was very different . Why was there so much quiet hostility in her home?

Blindly she raced forward through the

darkness as Fen bounded confidently ahead of her. Their passage became more treacherous. The rocks under her feet were slippery and Fen was guiding her towards the ravine, where the river raged beneath a sheer drop. Alva's heart sank and realization dawned. This was where she had been in her dream. Was it a prophecy? Had she seen her own death? Her mind told her to stop and turn back, but her heart and feet were dragged along by the silver outline of Fenrir ahead.

Alva began to run faster, trying to get past the point where she had fallen in her dream, and on to safety higher up. But—as if the gods were pulling her by strings, laughing at her—she felt the anticipated root catch on her shoe, lost her footing, and hurtled forward, towards the edge of the ravine. She knew what was coming. She'd seen it already. She was falling. She would become water and wind. The river yawned up at her . . .

But as quickly as she had been falling, Alva felt her body jerk and a sharp tug against her back. The black rocks and raging waters still seemed to reach up, yet they were not getting any closer. She heard a muffled noise behind her. Turning slowly, she saw Fenrir, his sharp fangs glinting in the light of the moon. He had her cloak between his teeth, and his paws rooted to the ground. Half Alva's body was hanging free over the edge of the cliff, but Fenrir dug his claws into the earth, growling as he slowly paced backwards, dragging her towards the safety of solid ground. She used her hands to scramble back over the edge and the two collapsed, wheezing and exhausted. Fenrir had saved her.

Alva gasped, pulling the wolf over to her by the scruff of his neck and burying her face in his soft, thick fur. 'You're always one step ahead, my silver saviour.' Fenrir turned two watery dark eyes upwards, nudging his muzzle against her cheek. She and Fen had beaten the Fates; death would not take her today.

She took a moment to catch her breath, as her chest was aching and she could taste fear in her mouth. Clambering back to her feet, she urged Fenrir on.

'Come on, boy. You've got the monk's scent. We need to get there before the others.' He turned, and in an instant became a flash of light between the trees ahead. Her canine guardian knew the way, and now Alva must follow.

Hidden in Plain View

As the dense forest thinned out, a wall of stone reared up out of the gloom. Alva and Fenrir reached a circular clearing, tucked beneath the huge crag in the mountainside. A snake of smoke hovered in the centre, creeping out of the embers of a dying fire. 'They were here!' Alva felt her heart beat faster again, this time in excitement. 'Well done, Fen,' she said, ruffling the wolf's head. 'You got us here, and we're first on the scene.'

Alva looked across the clearing, adjusting her vision to the half-light. Now she must swoop like an eagle, scanning the ground. Her sharp eyes must pick out the clues, if they were to solve the mystery announced by the stranger in the Jarl's hall tonight.

While her uncle was still locked in conversation with Jarl Erik, carefully navigating traditions and expectations, she would be first to test the truth of the monk's tale. The whole village would be amazed by her skills, and her uncle and mother would be drawn together in their celebration of her—no longer would Brianna accuse Magnus of filling her head with useless riddles. She could just imagine them all huddled around the table, laughing, and her uncle telling her how quick and clever she was.

At the edges of the spluttering fire, Alva could make out two flattened patches where the men had slept. She walked over slowly, and crouched down. Charred bones lay strewn around the fire pit, and a leather drinking pouch was discarded nearby. They had eaten and drunk, then slept.

She pressed herself closer to the ground. Alva had learnt from Uncle Magnus that to be a true investigator meant you had to examine lots and lots of seemingly boring detail. If she was to be the best investigator in Kilsgard she must look for clues—no matter how small or unimportant they might seem. She brushed the tangle of matted red hair out of her eyes and focused.

There, in the bracken, a shard of white. Nothing extraordinary. A humble toothpick, but further evidence that the men had camped here. She carefully placed the slither of bone inside her pouch, and turned towards the rear of the fire.

Now here was something interesting. Where one of the men had slept, Alva could see that the ground was disturbed. Perhaps this was where the monk's companion had slept. She drew closer, and there, within the clump of soil, something bright and liquid shimmered. Was that blood? From there, two parallel lines—thin ridges in the wet earth as if two hard objects had been dragged along the ground—ran off towards a clump of large shrubs nearby. She followed them, and found another clue behind the bushes, outlined in the dark earth. Hoofmarks. The two drag lines stopped next to them. A body must have been dragged here and carried off on horseback. She would need Fen and his supernatural sense of smell to find the rider.

Calling him to her side, Alva picked up a clump of earth from where the horse prints were deepest. She had trained Fenrir to follow scents since he was a cub, so held the soil to the wolf's nose and said, 'Fen, this is the new scent. Go and return.' The wolf was gone in an instant.

As Alva turned to survey the silent space, something else gleamed in the dim light. She'd missed it at first, but now she saw it trodden into the soil. It gleamed white, like the toothpick, but bigger and brighter. And unlike the toothpick it had four edges, was about two fingers in length and one in width. It seemed to have been buried in the earth, crushed by the horse's hooves. Crawling on her hands and knees, she touched the surface. Smooth, creamy-coloured—made of bone, perhaps? Even in the darkness she could see that shapes and symbols were carved all over its surface. Was this part of the casket? Running her hands gently around the edges, Alva prized it up from the ground. It was very thin, only the width of her smallest nail.

Dusting the soil from the surface, her fingertips walked their way cautiously over the object. Runes. She could feel their outlines. The symbols that surrounded her life. Her father had tied a piece of carved runic bone around her neck the day she was born, and she wore it still. The single symbol ᚠ. It meant fehu, wealth or riches, because to her parents Alva was the greatest treasure of all. While her mother had treated her like a precious gemstone to be kept safe within the family chest, her father had seen his daughter as a jewel to be worn proudly, like a magnificent brooch. He wanted Alva to experience what he experienced and see the world like he saw it.

There were too many runes carved on this piece for her to make sense of them. Holding it up to her eyes, she examined the object. It was a small, carved panel of bone. On one side it was smooth, but on the other a sequence of shapes and symbols were arranged in lines. It carried a message. This must be part of the casket the monk had been translating, what they had been following to find their 'treasures untold'. A secret message leading to fortune! This was unbelievable, and Alva had been the one to find it.

The English earl must have dropped this part of the casket as he was dragged away in the night. She had found the most important clue! What to do next though? The heavy weight of realization sank to the bottom of her stomach—

Uncle Magnus wouldn't be delightedly raising cups of mead at her discovery. He'd be furious when he realized she had overheard his interrogation and then raced ahead to Giant's Finger. And her mother was terrified whenever Alva left the house. She already thought it was Magnus's influence that was driving the girl into dangerous situations. She would punish her, and Magnus would be so angry. As if her thoughts were conjuring reality, Alva heard footsteps racing towards the clearing and her uncle's gravelly voice riding on the wind.

Simultaneously, a sharp, piercing cry shattered the eerie silence of the clearing, and a heavy weight descended on her shoulder.

'Alva bad!'

The shrill voice was right inside her ear. Alva reeled backwards, but she knew who this was. Hraf, her uncle's all-seeing pet raven.

Magnus had been training him for years, and he had been an ever-watchful presence in Alva's life, always following her, always seeing what the grown-ups couldn't. And that voice! Alva knew ravens were the cleverest of birds, sidekicks of the god of wisdom, Odin. She also knew that some could learn to speak with a human voice.

But Uncle Magnus had taught this blasted bird phrases designed to catch her out: 'Alva bad,' 'No, Alva,' 'I see you,' 'Alva gone' . . . Who needed the Norns—the three goddesses who spun the strands of each person's life—to twist your fate, when you had a black sky-rider to follow your every move? Why couldn't Alva's uncle trust her, like her father had? He would let her find her own adventures, but Magnus didn't like her being alone on her expeditions and had this beady-eyed spy follow her. 'I see you. Alva bad . . .' Hraf called out, over and over, as he whirled above the clearing.

The footsteps picked up their pace and Alva heard her uncle shout out in a confused voice, 'Are you here, girl?' There was no point hiding. The bird had found her. She walked over to the remains of the fire, but not until she had carefully and guiltily tucked the piece of carved bone into her pouch, out of sight of Hraf.

'I'm here, Uncle,' she said, in the meekest voice she could muster.

A group of men strode into the clearing. At the front was her uncle. Magnus was not the tallest or most impressive of Viking men, but he had presence. While others had arms the size of tree trunks or beards as thick as an oak in spring, Magnus was rather slight and his beard was thin, wispy and long, yet perfectly kept. Woven into its greying strands were gemstones and amulets Magnus had collected on his travels: amber from Russia, amethyst from Constantinople, jet from England. While other Viking men wore the finest furs and decorated themselves in silver, he went everywhere in his travelling cloak, which despite its many journeys, was clean as the day it was woven. He didn't have the eyes of a man set on heroism and battle, but clear, blue pools that drew you in and made you think of the passing of the ages.

Alva thought he was the most impressive man in Kilsgard. She loved him very much, particularly now her father was not there for her. But at this moment Uncle Magnus was not looking at her kindly. Alva's stomach knotted around itself as he stared straight at her with those knowing blue eyes.

Hraf landed on his master's shoulder, and clicked his beak angrily in her direction. Magnus took three large, deliberate steps towards his niece, and grabbed her by the arm. 'Alva,' he breathed in a low voice. 'What in the name of Odin are you doing here? This is the business of the Jarl. It is not for little girls to meddle in such matters.' His grip on her arm tightened.

Behind her uncle, she saw men in arms—the men of the Jarl. Their axes glinted in the half-light as they smiled in approval at Magnus's stern words to this reckless child. Her arm hurt as he squeezed it, and she felt the pressure constrict in her chest. He loved her—she knew that—but he could get very angry with her when she broke away on her adventures. 'I'm so sorry, uncle,' Alva whispered. She caught his eye, and mouthed at him: 'But I found clues. Good clues.' Magnus stared at her for a long moment, then he loosened his grasp. Turning so he was out of sight of the waiting karls, he gave her a slight smile. The conflicting sensations of fear and affection rushed through her. Was he proud, or was he livid with her? In an instant he had returned to the role of scolding father-figure.

'It is only my niece, good men,' he bellowed. 'She will be reprimanded at home for her foolishness at being out on a night of danger. She's been quite the reckless tearaway since Bjorn went a-Viking. Go and wait for me over there, girl,' he said, gesturing to the rocky wall at the back of the clearing. 'Right now I must turn my attention to this place.'

Once again, Magnus's focus shifted. Alva had vanished from his mind, and in her place were sets of clues, winding around one another and forming a story. Hraf flew up into a tree and settled to preening himself. Alva was no longer their concern. The armed men relaxed, leant against the trees, and pulled drinking pouches from their belts. But while they eased themselves, her uncle narrowed his piercing eyes, and began his own descent upon the rich treasure-hoard of clues.

'If the monk's story is true,' Magnus muttered, 'it will be written on the earth.'

Alva was always impressed by her uncle when he conducted his investigations. His calm, steady gaze never wavered. Even as he touched his finger to the red liquid where Alva guessed the second man had slept, and as he followed the trail to the horse's prints, he showed no sign that anything was untoward. He was measuring everything, storing it in his mind-hoard; collecting information, like a magpie. Throughout this process he did not raise his eyes from the ground and ignored Alva completely.

As she watched, he drew something from the worn leather bag slung round his waist. This bag had been across the seas, to the edges of the world, and back again. In it, Magnus stored many special devices he had acquired on his travels. He had navigation tools from men in the deserts, rune stones from Swedish seers, and writing implements from his time spent with monks.

Now he was taking out his strange glass that made the things he saw through it twice their size. It fascinated Alva, but she was never allowed to touch it as Magnus said it was most precious, and had come across sea and land to Kilsgard safely. One moment in Alva's adventurous hands and he worried its delicate transparent disc might meet its end. When in the past she had questioned him about it, Magnus had just said 'there is wisdom in other parts of the world, that we know nothing of.' He was always so elliptical—not like her father, who spoke to her as an adult from as early as Alva could remember.

She held back in the shadows near the rock face, nervously touching the piece of bone she had concealed in her own leather pouch. She desperately wanted to tell Magnus she had found it. She wanted to pore over its symbols with him, late into the night. But she wouldn't interrupt him now, not when he had looked at her with an expression like Thor's hammer had smashed him sideways. And besides, the karls were still here. Alva would have to wait.

A noise reached her across the breeze. It was extremely quiet, but she recognized it at once. Fenrir. His howl came from the other side of the mountain ridge, down by the water. Had he found something? Her uncle, usually so quick-witted, was still focused on the ground, and the babble of the noisy karls had drowned out the wolf's howl. But she knew it was Fen, calling her. Her uncle and Hraf couldn't care less about her right now. She could creep away, as long as she was silent.

Slowly rounding the back of the rock, Alva felt her way along its jagged edges. This really was unforgivable, to disobey her uncle twice in one evening. But Fenrir had followed the scent. Perhaps he was in danger right now, confronting the dark attacker alone. She must get to him.

Once she had moved behind the rock, Alva saw that the horse's hooves had left a clear track, where they had churned up the earth. The prints were deep, which meant the horse had a heavy load. Fenrir's call cut through the air a second time, and Alva quickened her step towards it. Soon she was running down the side of Giant's Finger, trying not to tumble on the steep incline. Through the blanket of trees she could just make out the banks of the river below, sparkling in the moonlight. A few more paces and her shoes crunched the familiar sand of the bay, beneath her soles.

Alva had visited this shore many times in her life. The river was shallow here, and, carved on the rocky bed, were ancient pictures. Images of ships, of her ancestors, of runes. Who knew how old they were? Surely they were put here when the giants still lived in Kilsgard. Her father had brought her here before he'd left to go a-Viking the last time, and together they had woven stories around these pictures. He had told her that he had to go away, but she should always come back here if she wanted to be close to him. It was a special place for her.

Fenrir ran to meet her, but he was alone. No horse, no rider, no lost English warrior. She could see that the horse's hooves went as far as the water's edge, then disappeared. Clever, Alva thought. *The rider knows Kilsgard well. He could make his horse's scent disappear in the water, and simply ride upstream, downstream, or to the other bank. We will never find him now.*

She sat down to catch her breath, rubbing the gritty sand between her fingers. Her father's strong, rugged face hovered in her mind as she recalled their last visit to this cove together. A pain crept across her chest. It was familiar. It was sorrow. She missed him. It had been nine months now, and he had left in such a hurry.

Their last words to each other had been harsh.

Alva had been angry with him for leaving her stuck here between her smothering mother and domineering uncle. She needed him, but instead of sending him away with words of love, she had spoken unkindly. Now winter had come, and the men should have been back from their journeys. None of the thirty men who had left with her father for the city of Constantinople had come back. Alva knew he may never return. Cold, full drops of rain landed on her head and ran down her face, mixing with the warm tears streaming from her eyes.

Rain. That was not good. Rain would wash away the tracks. It would hide the clues. It would disturb the men and her uncle, and she would be missed. Grabbing Fenrir, Alva began the sharp ascent back towards the clearing. The men's voices became louder with every step.

'We have to go, Magnus,' she heard one of the karls call. 'It's raining, and I've got no dry clothes left at the hall. If this jerkin gets soaked I'll be chilled for the day. And the Jarl will want us to return with news. We've already been too long, labouring over this dirt.'

'One more sample,' her uncle replied, his face still pressed close to the ground.

Alva rounded the top of the hill in time to see her uncle stand up and place a set of vials in his bag. He looked at her and saw Fenrir cowering behind. 'So the wolf is here too, is he? Alva, you and your pet should return home. I must take news of my investigations to Jarl Erik. We shall descend to the village together, and I will deal with you when I get back.'

Traipsing along in silence, Alva felt her hair getting heavy with rain water, and the soles of her shoes slipped over the rocks as Giant's Finger towered behind them.

The proud, pointed peak of the mountain jutted like a dagger, skywards towards Valhalla—home of the gods—as if announcing, 'This is the land of Vikings.'

Alva wanted to get her uncle alone, so she could show him the piece of casket, but he strode ahead with the karls. Partly, she felt she had done well to discover it, but deep down Alva knew she should have left the evidence for Magnus to find and inspect. She would be in such trouble for interfering, and as a result her mother would no doubt wrap her in swaddling to prevent her leaving the house again.

As the ground levelled out, the turfed roofs

of Kilsgard appeared in the distance. It was still dark, but a few lights were appearing throughout the town as early risers went to feed animals and begin chores. The group passed through a gateway, and saw Meginsalr flickering with light from inside. Magnus made towards it with the karls, but stopped, turning to Alva. In the half-light his eyes looked like glinting jet beads. 'You have done a bad thing tonight, girl, to go alone on your investigations. I understand what compels you, but your mother will have to hear of this. You know this will make things even more difficult between us all. First, you will be punished as she sees fit. Then we can talk about whatever it is you keep touching in your pouch.' He took the slightest glance at her waist, where she had her hand wrapped around the bone fragment. He really did see everything.

Alva wound back along the track to her hut, thinking about what she would say when her mother awoke. But on opening the door, she realized she wouldn't have to wait till morning.

'Alva!' Her mother's pale-white skin was etched with lines of worry as she jiggled a red-faced Ivan up and down in the darkness. Brianna reared up, mighty, in a flame of red hair and flashing green eyes. With a note of sadness beneath her fury, she whispered through gritted teeth: 'Daughter, I love you. But your adventurous spirit will be your undoing, and the undoing of all that love you.'

Then There Were None

Alva's mouth was watering. Ivan shovelled another hunk of bread into his hot little face, staring at her while he chewed and dribbled. Her stomach groaned. The punishment for her late-night adventure was a lengthy tongue lashing from her mother and no breakfast. She was also meant to stay within the hut for five days and nights, but Magnus had returned in the early hours of the morning and said he would need her to assist him. A small mercy, but one that had set her mother glowering around the kitchen like a newly sparked fire.

Ivan licked his lips and ran off to pester Brianna as her uncle strode menacingly towards the table. Despite having saved her from part of her punishment, Magnus was not in a kind mood when he sat down next to Alva on the bench. It rattled as he drew it towards the table, and Alva shrank smaller so as to avoid his glare.

'You did a very foolish thing last night, girl. I presume you followed me to the hall when the Jarl's men arrived? If so, you must have heard the alarming saga spun by the monk, Edmund of Lindisfarne.'

'Yes, I'm sorry uncle. But what a thrilling tale—'

Her uncle interrupted angrily. 'In that case you will know that a man was taken by force in the night. And of all nights you chose that one to go adventuring in the mountains. You are a reckless and wild child. By the gods, you still have the branches of the mountain tangled in your hair! You will need to be far more presentable if we are to visit Meginsalr.'

Alva sat up with excitement, 'I'm going to the Jarl's hall?!'

'This is not a prize, girl,' her uncle snapped. 'You will need to come with me and show him that object you have in your pouch. But first, you must show it to me.'

She could feel her cheeks glowing red. 'I would have shown it to you sooner, but with the jarl's men around . . .' Her voice trailed off as she brought the bone fragment out from the knot of yarn, pebbles, leaves, and buttons congealed at the bottom of her pouch. When her mother had finally stopped shouting at Alva in the early hours, and let her go to bed, she had taken out the object to wipe the dirt from it. It was still mucky, but the rows of repeating runes were now much clearer on the surface.

'Do you know what this is?' Magnus said to her, taking the piece of bone from her hands.

'Yes, uncle,' she replied. 'I heard the stranger tell of a casket with clues that would lead to an incredible treasure. I guess this is part of the box?'

He didn't reply, but turned his eyes towards the lines of runes that were etched skilfully on the fragment in his hands. His face was pale. Suddenly he leapt from his seat. Alva craned her neck to see what had given her uncle such a shock. What could have upset him so much? 'Brianna,' he called anxiously. Her mother dropped her ladle, with a clatter, into the large pot she was stirring on the fire.

'What is it?' she said brusquely. 'The broth is boiling over.'

'Come here,' he replied.

'You'll have to wait,' said her mother, wiping her hands on her apron. After a raging tirade first thing, when she and Magnus had argued over Alva being allowed out of the house, she had hardly spoken a word to either of them since rising. Instead she was purposely ignoring them; cooking, cajoling Ivan, and noisily bustling around the hearth at the other end of the hut.

Alva was now fixated on the white fragment on the table in front of her, which was lying brightly in a shaft of sunlight that glanced through the open shutters.

'If your mother doesn't want to know, then so be it,' Magnus said lowering his voice. 'We will work quietly on this together—a secret mission just for you and me. Look at these runes, Alva. Do you see anything?' Her uncle's eyes were wide, and he looked worried.

Magnus edged closer to her and took her by the hand. He placed her finger on top of a single rune. She could feel his palms were clammy. Suddenly her sense of excitement was replaced with one of fear.

'What letter is that, Alva?' he asked.

'It looks to me like fehu,' she replied, but then she saw the symbol next to it—a small triangle-shape. Alva knew these two signs well. Her father had scratched them over and over for her. 'By Freya! That's my name.'

ᚠ △

'Now look here,' said her uncle. He pointed to another rune.

'It's mannaz, the rune for man,' said Alva.

'Yes, but look at the rune next to it,' Magnus replied. There was a circle with a line through it next to the man rune. 'This was your father's way of referring to me. As young boys we talked of being two halves of a whole—one man in two parts.'

ᛗ ϕ

'And here,' he said, lowering his voice so he couldn't be heard above Ivan's happy shrieks and Brianna's clattering around. He pointed to the rune othalan.

'The rune for home?' Alva asked. Beside it was another strange symbol; an apple. Magnus placed his finger over that.

ᚠᛟ

'This is the symbol of Idunna, the Goddess of the Eternal Spring, who alone could pick the sacred apples and provide an endless feast for the gods. Your father said your mother was the goddess of his home. So this was how he wrote her name.' Alva's mind began to replay a long-forgotten memory- her father chasing her mother around the hut, the two of them laughing, with a half-eaten apple. Her heart ached for a moment.

They sat in silence, looking at the repeating patterns of their names, etched one after the other in lines across the bone fragment.

'These are our runes. This is from Father,' Alva said slowly.

Magnus looked at her and nodded. 'It seems so.'

'We must tell Mother.'

They looked towards the hearth where Brianna was angrily scrubbing Ivan. He had soiled himself and there was mess everywhere. 'The news that this casket has something to do with your father will upset her,' said Magnus. 'She doesn't yet know all the details about our investigations in the forest, and we still have more to discover. I think we should keep this to ourselves for a little longer while we investigate. Now we know that Bjorn is somehow involved in this, the mystery gets more unsettling at every step. I think we need to speak with the man who found this casket. Perhaps he has news of Bjorn's whereabouts.'

'It's been nearly a year,' Alva replied sadly. 'It is too much to hope that my father will return to Kilsgard.'

'And yet,' Magnus answered, 'here he speaks directly to us. The monk must know something. Jarl Erik gave him safe haven last night, so perhaps he can tell us where he got the casket. He may even recall some of the other runes.'

He grabbed his cloak then looked over at Alva.

'Well, come on,' he said. 'You will have to pick the bramble out of your shabby hair as we go. By the gods, you need to take more care, girl. You could bathe occasionally.' He strode out of the room and Alva scuttled quickly behind. They could hear Brianna shouting angrily at the door as it closed off her muffled her cries.

***

The outline of Meginsalr glowed in the bright wintery sunlight. Kilsgard was coming to life after a fretful night, but the daily sounds of sweeping floors, lowing cattle, and busy wagons were slowly filling the air. Alva felt a thrill of excitement rush through her. Magnus was including her in his investigations for the first time. She had a slight spring in her step as she approached the Jarl's hall.

Above the gable of the wide oak doors was a carved figure; Jormungand, the World Serpent, writhing across the upper beams and biting onto his tail. While he held tight, the world would continue. If he let go, the chaos of Ragnarök—the end of the world—would begin.

Alva had passed through these doors a number of times in her life. Once, she was allowed to watch as her uncle gave testimony in front of the Jarl for the life of a man caught stealing. Uncle Magnus was often called upon by Jarl Erik for his wisdom and careful assessment of crimes. But Alva was awed by the massive space every time she walked into Meginsalr's lofty, vaulted hall. The roof was four times as high as that of her own hut, and around the sides benches were covered with lush furs and woollen blankets. At the centre was a huge hearth-fire, and standing there, warming his hands, was the Jarl.

Though not as tall as her uncle, the Jarl was broader and wider than Magnus. As a young man he had been a fierce warrior, but too many roast pigs and too much mead had shrunken him and given him a soft stomach that stuck out over his leather belt. Two round, red cheeks perched above his full brown beard, and twinkling eyes peered out through a mass of dark, braided hair. He did not scare Alva.

'Magnus,' Erik bellowed from the fireplace, his beard juddering. 'And youngling Alva, too. What a night it has been. None of us have slept well in the hall. The thought of a criminal roaming Giant's Finger has set the fire of vengeance burning in the heart of many of the men here. They want to find this villain and punish him. Have you discovered any more since we spoke?'

Magnus shook off his cloak and walked over. 'Yes, Jarl Erik,' he replied, handing over the fragment of casket. 'I'm so sorry I didn't bring this to your attention last night, but my niece here did something very disobedient. Don't worry, she has been sorely reprimanded—but she went ahead of me to the site where the man was taken and found this.'

'That was a reckless thing to do, Alva,' said the Jarl. 'You are so like your father. We could never keep him from wandering alone in the mountains either, could we, Magnus?' Chuckling, he clapped a huge, weather-worn hand on Magnus's shoulder. 'So you found this, Alva?'

Her cheeks burnt red with a mix of pride and embarrassment. She mumbled towards her shoes, 'I did.'

'But what is this?' Erik looked down at the piece of bone, turning it over to explore its surfaces in the flickering firelight. 'The casket?' he enquired of Magnus. 'Here are runes—but some I know, some I do not.'

'It is but part of the casket. I think it's the lid,' Magnus replied. 'It must have come loose as the warrior was dragged away in the night. It fell into the mud and Alva here found it. She only showed it to me for the first time this morning, and I came straight to you. We cannot decode the runes yet.' He glanced down at the floor as he said this.

Alva knew this meant he was lying, which, of course, he was.

'It seems to be encrypted,' her uncle continued,

'and this is only part of the message. We need to know what else was written on this strange box. Naturally we will need to speak with the monk.'

'Naturally,' Erik replied. 'We put him to rest in the outhouse. He was exhausted from his ordeal and did not trust to sleep in here with all the karls. I don't blame him! We have not seen him yet this morning. Go wake him and tell him he can eat in here with us if he would like. We're having mutton stew.' Erik slapped his chops enthusiastically at the thought.

Alva followed Uncle Magnus through the hall to the rear door, which backed on to a yard. Around the periphery was a cluster of small wooden huts. Some were used to house workmen or servants, while others contained beasts. Magnus saw the door of the central hut was still closed, so walked towards it. After banging his fist against the side, he pushed the door open and they walked in. The space was empty.

'Uncle,' Alva said, pointing nervously at the floor. The hay that the monk had used as a bed was disturbed. 'It looks like someone was struggling here,' she whispered anxiously. Magnus bent down and looked closely at the ground. The hay was churned up in mounds, and there was the red stain of blood scattered in drops across the floorboards. The air turned still as both held their breath.

'This is very serious, Alva. I don't think the monk left here willingly. I think he, like the English warrior, has been removed by force. We must tell Erik. His household will be under suspicion now, as Edmund of Lindisfarne has been seized from his property when he was promised safety.'

But Alva was distracted. She had noticed something on the back wall of the hut. 'Look here,' she said striding over the floor.

'Alva!' Magnus shrieked, 'you are walking straight through the evidence.' But then he saw what she was pointing at. Runes were carved into the wooden panels on the back wall. 'By Thor!' he murmured. 'You really are becoming quite the investigator, Alva.' Drawing closer, he pulled the strange circular glass from his leather pouch. He also drew out his writing tablet and stylus.

'These must be the missing runes,' Alva said excitedly. Looking over her shoulder she could see that her uncle was already scribbling small versions of the symbols onto his wax board. 'But they can't be complete, can they?' she continued. 'Surely the monk wouldn't have known all the runes, he must have been carving these from memory. I wonder if we can trust them . . .'

'Stand back, girl,' Magnus grumbled at her. 'You are blocking the light. Give me some time to get them down. Why don't you look around the floor? See if we have missed anything.'

Alva walked across the small space, casting her eyes over the hay. To the left on the wall were wooden shelves full of farming implements, buckets, and building materials. Cobwebs and dust covered most of the items, but tucked next to a rusty knife was a small bag. It was not dusty. Alva took it down. It was a battered, old leather pouch. Lifting the flap she felt inside, drawing out something brittle. 'Uncle, what's this?' she called across the room.

She held the contents of the bag up in the light. 'Where did you find that?' Magnus asked, taking the scroll from her hand. 'You know what this is, Alva?! It's parchment. Animal skin. Monks use it to write down their sacred texts, and anything else they want to be remembered beyond their lifetimes.'

He unfurled the thin roll, and Alva saw symbols scribbled over the surface. She knew what this was: Latin. The language the Christians used. They did not scratch their letters into stones, or leather, or bone—they wrote onto the skins of sheep which had been scraped thin and tied together within leather covers.

Many Vikings did not understand the importance of these *books*, but Alva's father and uncle had shown her some and taught her to respect them. They held the knowledge of ages and the stories of people from all over the world. Bjorn in particular used to tell her many fantastical tales he had read in books while on his travels, in which brave knights romanced beautiful princesses, and sought hidden treasure on great quests.

Amidst the scribbles of black gall ink in front of her now, Alva could see there was a diagram. A green shape with blue edging, and individual small buildings painted across it. 'What does that show?' she asked, pointing at the picture.

'I think it is a map,' Magnus replied.

'Do you mean it is a picture of land?' Alva asked quizzically.

'Yes. They are extremely rare, but in some parts

of the world, travellers have plot their journeys as a picture, to show the limits of kingdoms, the coastlines, and the pathways from town to town.'

He looked more closely, and as he read the word written in largest script above a particular structure he took a step back.

'Well, well. This is a map showing a route from Edmund's monastery of Lindisfarne to the great city of Constantinople. This is an extraordinary thing for a monk to own! Why would he have this in his possession?'

Alva took the parchment from Uncle Magnus and looked at it carefully. The blue areas must be sea, she figured, and the green areas land. 'What a thing!' she said, mystified. 'Imagine if our men had such guidance when they went a-Viking. You would be able to navigate the waters like a seagull looking down from above. Do you think the monk has travelled this long route?'

'Well, he mentioned being on a long journey with his companion. Perhaps it was on his way to Constantinople that he encountered Bjorn. Your father was set for that golden place, looking to secure wealth through trading along the route. Alva, this gets clearer and yet more opaque with every moment. I fear this is only the start of the saga.'

Honouring the Gods

'He's gone,' Magnus said, striding into Meginsalr.

Jarl Erik dropped the meat he had been eating into its bowl, and wiped a streak of fat from his chin. 'The monk?' he mumbled, through half-chewed food.

'Yes,' Magnus answered. 'The hut was disturbed and there was evidence of a struggle. Erik, this is very bad. Someone has come into your property and seized a man who sought refuge in your hall. The people of Kilsgard are already terrified there is a threatening presence in the mountains, but now it has crept here, into our town.'

Erik pushed his bench back from the table with a loud scraping noise, and moved towards Magnus. But before he could say anything, a shrill, croaking voice cut in from the dark shadows at the back of the hall.

'A threat has beset us.'

The voice made Alva shudder.

'Two men taken in the night. This is the work of Loki for sure. He has cast a curse on Kilsgard, and is taking its visitors. Soon he will take us too. We are cursed . . .'

The outline of a figure crept into view as the speaker moved closer to the hearth. But Alva knew this voice regardless. It was Sigrunn, seer of Kilsgard, slaughterer and sacrifice-giver. As she moved into the light, her distorted figure and twisted face looked like Alva's night terrors. She stooped as she walked, and her full-length cloak rustled with the bunches of herbs, animal bones, and amulets she had woven into its weft. Sigrunn had just one eye. In place of the second was a scarred hole where it had been removed, in service of Odin, the one-eyed god. The eye that remained was cloudy, and flecked with silver shapes. White bristles emerged from her chin, while grey strands of hair crept from under Sigrunn's black head scarf. Her face was lined with the passage of time, and painted with chalk and charcoal, making her all the more ghoulish.

'Hear me,' she announced to the hall. 'Hear me and heed me. Kilsgard is beset by strange events. Events that even our wise crow of the west, Magnus Gutharson, cannot explain with his wisdom from overseas. It is clear that we need to call upon the help of our gods to rid us of this terror. The great god of mischief and mayhem, Loki, is behind these strange occurrences and we must make sacrifice to him so he will show us kindness. When he is satisfied with our gifts, Kilsgard will again be safe.'

She turned her single eye on Jarl Erik. 'You must arrange for every family to bring a sacrifice to the hall at sundown. It must be a worthy gift. Something each family values and needs. Only then will Loki stop his games.' Alva caught her breath. Would they have to bring an animal? Which one?

Erik began to speak, but Sigrunn lifted one brittle, bent, bony finger to her lips.

'Hush. This needs action, not words. I charge you with this. On your house and on your head be this sacrifice, Jarl Erik. You need to protect your people. You need a sacrifice.'

With more haste than seemed possible for a woman of her age, she swept from the room.

Magnus turned to the hearth and spat, making the flames flicker in his disgust. 'That woman is cruel, Erik.' He said. 'It is unnecessary for the people to sacrifice good beasts for this. We still have to conduct our investigations, and stirring the town into a frenzy of fear will not serve anyone. I urge you to ignore her and let me continue my work.'

'No, Magnus,' Erik replied sternly. 'Sigrunn is terrifying, but we all know she communes with the gods. To anger her is to anger them. We must perform the ancient rituals, regardless of what your travels have taught you. It is part of Kilsgard. It is the Viking way. The gods must be appeased.' Alva could feel the nails on her fingers digging into the palms of her hands as she clenched her fists with silent rage.

'You follow what this mad old crone instructs, but I will not,' Magnus responded. 'Alva and I have something real and useful to do. We will solve this riddle and we will capture this night thief. And we will use our minds and our eyes to do so.'

Her uncle's words, 'Alva and I', brought a fresh flood of warm excitement to her, but she quickly scurried away from Jarl Erik, following

Magnus as he stormed out of the hall. 'Uncle, I don't like Seer Sigrunn's sacrifices. Will we have to give something, too?' Fenrir had followed Alva to the hall and was waiting by the door, being eyed nervously by passers-by. As they walked towards home he fell into step behind them, and for a moment Alva feared that she might have to give her beloved wolf up for sacrifice. She went cold at the thought.

'Yes, I imagine we will. Though we have little we can spare. This is why your father left us to go a-Viking, Alva, as he worried that we do not have enough wealth or possessions. To lose even one beast will affect us through the winter. You know that I cling to Odin and the gods, but surely you can see these senseless rituals are not what we need right now. There are many others in the village who are struggling, too, and can poorly afford to give up valuable animals for slaughter during these cold months. Come. We have to examine the evidence. If our minds work fast we may be able to bring about a solution before sundown.' Alva felt a great sense of urgency. She didn't want to see any of her animals die at the cruel hands of this wicked crone. They had to set their minds to work, fast.

***

Back at home, with Fenrir slouched comfortably under the table and Hraf perched on the back of Magnus's chair. Alva and Magnus spread the clues they'd gathered across the oak table. Ivan played with a small wooden wolf their father had carved for him before he left, as Brianna grumpily presented bowls of stew. She was still resolutely silent, quietly raging at Magnus for taking Alva from the home without her permission. Alva wondered how long her feisty mother would be able to keep up this pretence. Surely she was curious at the array of strange objects spread over the table?

Alva sat with her uncle, spooning hot, sloppy nourishment into her mouth. She was famished. In front of them lay the bone fragment, Magnus's sketches of the monk's carvings, and Edmund's parchments. A lot to decipher.

'I can't make any sense of any of it,' Alva said, banging her spoon on the side of her wooden bowl. 'I can see runes I know, but I can't see a message. And the monk's mad scrawlings on that calf skin . . . I've no idea where to start there!'

'Okay,' Magnus said calmly. 'I can assist with that. My Latin is not excellent, but I have learnt enough to get the sense of what is recorded here.' He ran his finger around the edge of the green image of land, settling on the small ink letters surrounding it. 'The monk has kept some sort of account of journeys here, I am sure of it. Look.' He pointed at a small red outline that looked like a hall, depicted near the top of the parchment. 'The notation says "Lindisfarne" and the smaller writing underneath reads "home". The monk Edmund was from this monastery.'

Alva interjected, 'So he begins in Lindisfarne, but then this line shows he travelled south.'

Magnus ran his finger down the parchment. 'All along the way, he has added notes. Look, near to this stretch of water—he writes how they waited two days for a ship to take them to Gaul, and that the crossing was treacherous. And over here.' He pointed to another red building, on the other side of the stretch of blue water. 'The monk has written "here, Abbot Denis gave us room and food. We prayed with the brothers". This is an important document.'

'But does it say anything about Father? About where they may have met him, or where they got the box?' Alva asked earnestly.

Magnus turned over a few leaves of parchment, until he came to a third map. This showed more brown and less blue, so Alva guessed it must be a map of the inland. Magnus bent his face close to the small script, slowly reading the monk's scribbles in the margin. 'There's no reference to Bjorn, but this is interesting . . . Here, by a town in Francia, the monk has written the word "Viccingi". He records that he met with Vikings, so perhaps this means he met with Bjorn?'

Alva looked at the little Latin word: Viccingi. She didn't like it. How could one little word describe the strong men of her village, men like her father, who went out on the dangerous seas, searching for sustenance for their people over the hard winter months. Their brave adventurers were the fiercest in the world—her father told her that. They were so much more than that little scribble. But that was all the monk had written.

Magnus was now looking at another page.

There were more maps, but they were less ornate; just lines and names linked together. Alva saw a red trail of ink moving up the page.

'Does this mean they came north, uncle?' she asked, tracing the line with her finger.

'I think so, Alva,' he replied. 'I think this is where our bold monk picked up the trail from our riddling box. And here is what he was after.' As he turned to yet another page, Alva saw a final map, and something strange. An image of a man. It looked so real! The face was pink and fleshy, the clothes were bright, embroidered, rich . . . It was as if the figure could step out of the page.

Alva stepped away from the parchment. In the sunlight, she could see the figure's head was surrounded by a ring of pure gold. 'Who is that?' she asked nervously. 'And why is he ringed in gold? Is he a god?'

'I have spent time with Christians on my travels. They only worship one God, but they also honour a mother, a son, a spirit, and a whole collection of the dead. They call them saints. I think this is a saint. And look, Alva—above the man's head is one word: "Treasure".'

Ivan suddenly let out a scream. He was sat on the floor of the hut, with the wooden wolf

lying in front of him. The leg had snapped off.
Brianna rushed to the mass of crying red hair,
swooping him off the ground, and looked down
sadly at the broken toy.

'Another piece of your father gone,' she
mumbled quietly, then swept Ivan off to their
bed. Alva felt a tug at her heart as she thought of
her father sat by the fire, whittling the wood to
make the little broken toy, and it pulled her out
of her trance.

She had been so excited that Magnus was
asking her opinion, working through the
evidence with her help, that for a short moment
she had forgotten the pain her father's absence
left imprinted on their home every day. Plus,
she had been transfixed by the picture of what
looked like a living god, on the pages of animal
skin. At Ivan's cry, Magnus too was roused to
action. He grabbed the parchment, rolled it up
and pushed it to one side.

'Alva,' he said, 'we can only get so far with the
monk's scribbles, but we have our own tongue
here to decipher. We can decode these runes. In
fact, if it was your father who scratched them, I
think that we alone can understand them. We've
seen our names on the lid, but what other runes

were there on the casket? We should look at the monk's carvings.'

He pulled the tablet with his small etching over towards them. 'This is what I could see from the monk's scratchings on the wall. I think they may be incomplete and incorrect, memorized by a monk whose first language is English, and who writes in Latin, not in runes. But we must try. Now, child, you have a good understanding of the runes. Both your father and I have tried to impress their importance on you over the years, since we were both fortunate to have been taught the gift of reading them. Now's your chance to show me whether all we taught you entered your mind-hoard. Your turn Alva; tell me how we read these symbols.'

Alva thought back to the many times she had sat at this table with her father as he carved shapes into pieces of wood. With each carving he would recite poems, until Alva knew the stories and legends connected to each symbol by heart. 'Uncle,' she said, 'the runes are letters, but they are also words, and beyond that, they are stories.'

'Good,' Magnus answered. 'When we use these symbols they can work in different ways, and that is how the skilled user of runes can encrypt their messages. Sometimes a rune will be a simple letter, sometimes a word, and sometimes the reader will have to cast their minds further, to a web of hidden meanings. Now what has the monk written?'

They both focused on the lines, reading from right to left:

ᚠᛟᚱ ᚠ ᛟᚠ ᛏᚺᛖ ᚨ ᚱ ᛏᛟ ᚲᛁᛚᛊᚷᚨᚱᛞ

ᚹ ᛟᚠ ᚹᛖᛊᛏᛖᚱᚾ ᚠᛟᛖᛊ ᛚᛁᛖᛊ ᚺᛁᛞᛞᛖᚾ ᛁᚾ

ᚨ ᛞᚨᚱᚲ ᛈᛚᚨᚲᛖ ᚨᛏ ᛏᚺᛖ ᛒ

ᚠᚱᛟᛗ ᛃᚨᚱᛚ ᛖᚱᛁᚲᛊ ᚺᚨᛚᛚ ᚱ ᛏᛟ

ᚦᚠᛁᚾ ᚷᛖᚱ

ᚠᛟᛚᛚᛟᚹ

'I cannot read this, Uncle,' Alva said after a moment. 'I'm sure it is encrypted, as there are some parts that make no sense.'

'Indeed, Alva,' Magnus said thoughtfully. 'What words can you make out?'

After staring more intently for a moment, Alva's face lit up. 'Oh look,' she said, 'there is the name Kilsgard! So the opening directs the reader to our village!'

ᚲᛁᛚᛅᚷᚨᚱᛗ

'Good,' Magnus answered. 'There are also smaller words that stand out clearly. Look: "for, of, the, to"—they are directions.'

'I can see a name,' Alva squealed excitedly, 'Jarl Erik!'

ᛋᚠᚱᛚ ᛗᚱᛁᚲ

'Yes!' said Magnus, excitement creeping into his voice too. 'It says "from Jarl Erik's hall", and here is the shortened version of Giant's Finger— Thor's finger. These are certainly directions. Which runes are encoded, do you think, Alva?'

She scanned the runes, eliminating those that joined to make full words, names, or locations, and settled on a few that stood alone. 'The ones that are by themselves, perhaps they are meant to be read as words rather than as letters? What do you think?'

'I think you are right,' he replied, smiling at her. 'So now we've eliminated the runes we know, that leaves us with the encrypted ones. Here it reads "fehu ᚠ of the ansuz ᚠ". You must know what that means, girl?'

Alva thought for a moment. 'Treasures of the gods.'

'Good!' he replied. Now, you know what

this rune here means.' He gestured at the raidō
ᚱ rune.

'That means "journey", so it's saying the reader should journey to Kilsgard. But I really don't understand this next section.'

Magnus brought the circle of glass out from his pouch and focused it on one of the runes. 'This is the rune wunjō ᚹ, which means—'

Alva interrupted, 'It means "joy"!'

'Yes, "the joys of the Western foes". Alva,' said Magnus, 'I know what it is referring to.' He took a step back from the table and turned away from her. When he spoke again his voice was low and slow. Seeing her uncle's change in mood, Alva gripped the edge of the table and held her breath, waiting for him to continue. After a long pause he spoke.

'Alva, you have heard the many tales of my and your father's journeys to the distant land of the English, and to the island of Lindisfarne just last year. It is a strange place, nestled on the edge of the kingdom of the northern English, and it is entirely inhabited by weak, yet perilously rich, monks. Your father had heard of these undefended monk towns, on his travels, and brought news back to Jarl Erik. He spread the information to other jarls of the North and it was agreed to send a small set of ships to the island to investigate whether it was true that treasures were defended by peace-loving, unarmed men. Your father and I agreed to accompany the ships, since we knew some Latin and could represent the Jarl's interests.'

Alva interjected, 'I remember that you and Father were at odds when you returned. You argued in the weeks after you got back, and then Father went away again so suddenly . . . I never knew what had happened there.'

Magnus turned back towards Alva. He had a sad and distant look in his eyes. He sat down next to her and took her hand. 'Alva,' he said, 'when the men go a-Viking it can be a bloody and brutal business. Often we will travel for days on wild oceans, and when we reach the shore, the locals want to murder us and turn us away. When we set our sails for Lindisfarne we all had the wolf of battle in our bellies, and the thirst for gold made our mouths dry.

'As our boats climbed the shallow shores, we could see the monks fleeing, and they rang bells, escaping further inland. There had been men from our lands on this island before, and they were terrified when they saw our dragon-

prowed ships. Many of our men leapt onto the sand, hungry for slaughter, fame, and fortune. But your father and I knew where the Christians kept their wealth—in the main temple. They call this their "church".

'We went there directly, spilling no blood. Once we were in the sanctuary, however, we found three of the monks pulling a box from beneath a stone slab. They were startled, and two of them ran. The third lay down in front of the box, screaming in Latin, "Take me, not our treasure!". Your father pushed the man aside, and he struck his head on the stone altar. He moved no more. I reproached your father for his actions, but the two of us knew that we had found the most precious treasure the monks possessed, so he laid claim to it and took it to the ship. When we finally opened the box, we found some gold-encrusted books, and bones.

'We had secured a good haul of gold from the journey, so were not concerned that Jarl Erik would expect more from our expedition. Bjorn insisted we keep the box secret from the other men, since he knew they would be superstitious and say we should cast the bones into the sea. But we knew their true worth. Your father and

I remembered what we had learnt on our travels about the bones of saints: they are valued more highly than any treasure, since Christians think they can work wonders, and can take you directly to their god. To some, they are worth more than any pile of gold your mind can picture.'

'That sounds crazy,' Alva interrupted, shaking her head in disbelief, 'how can bones be worth more than gold?'

'They are called "relics",' Magnus replied, 'and they are thought to connect those on earth with those in the afterlife. I argued with your father about them, as I did not want to touch the remains of one of these Christian's saints, and felt we should show them to Jarl Erik. Bjorn wanted to keep them, sell them, and bring wealth to his family, since we were struggling then as we are now. He thought we could ransom the treasures back to the monks, perhaps, or we could sell the bones to other Christians on our travels, for huge sums. He felt the other men and the Jarl would not understand their value, and that he and I had found them alone, so they were rightfully ours.

'Bjorn became possessive and secretive about the bones. When we got back to Kilsgard he told me he had hidden them. He spoke very mysteriously about them when I asked him, saying the treasure would do more than bring us earthly riches; they would bring us riches of the heart and soul.

'I am a man who has travelled widely. I know the reputation our men have across Christian lands. We are called heathens, barbarians, and murderers. Just look at the blood sacrifice Sigrunn has in store for our town tonight— blood and violence runs deep through our legends. When I journey, I try to temper the men's bloodlust, but our lives and those of our people here in Kilsgard depend on our efforts, and if we want our place alongside the gods in Valhalla, we have to secure fame and glory. Nevertheless, I know we took something the monks valued very greatly, and I fear that now is our time to answer for it. I've been reluctant to tell anyone of this story, since it casts your father in a dark light. Even your mother was never told of this.'

Leaning closer to her uncle, Alva replied, 'My father brought about the death of one of those peace-loving monks, and he hid treasure from the Jarl?'

'Your father is a good man, but a complicated one. His head is always full of stories, fantasies, and quests. He loves you, Brianna, and Ivan deeply, but sometimes his thoughts and actions are hard to read. This is why we argued,' Magnus answered sadly. 'I was angry with your father for the events at Lindisfarne, but your mother was also angry. She felt you were becoming more reckless while we were away a-Viking, because Bjorn always gave you such freedom and treated you like his equal. She didn't want your father to go away again. Brianna felt he should stay here and encourage you to change your ways. I felt he should be honest with the Jarl before his departure . . . and so, we find ourselves in this situation now. We have been waiting nine months for Bjorn's intervention, and here it is!'

'What do you mean?' asked Alva, feeling confused.

'Your father carved the casket to show us— his family—where he had hidden the treasure. I still can't fully understand why. But it is clear that these riddles direct us to the "joys of the western foes", the bones of the saint. That is why the monk and English warrior came here, and that is why they are now missing. We have to solve these riddles and find the treasure your father has hidden for us. Then we can decide what to do with it.'

In Search of Gold

Alva leapt from her seat as a fist thudded on the door.

'Magnus,' a deep voice shouted, 'the Jarl needs you at the hall immediately. More chaos has come.'

Her uncle jumped up, the flame back in his eyes. 'What has happened now?' he asked, swinging the door open to reveal two of the Jarl's men, in full armour.

'Men have come to Kilsgard from Jarl Gudmund's lands, a day's ride from here. There is great unrest at the hall. The seer is calling for sacrifice and the people of the village are scared.'

Magnus turned to Alva. 'I must leave immediately. Put all the evidence in a bag and leave it here with your mother. Then come to meet me at the hall. Bring the wolf—we may need his special skills.' He took Hraf from the perch by the door and swept out of the hut.

Alva was left at the table, her head swimming with the stories her uncle had poured into it.

Her father had killed a man in Lindisfarne, and he had hidden treasure. She knew that in the many months her father had spent journeying abroad he would have done things he wouldn't want his daughter or wife to know about. But she had heard the monk Edmund speak, and he had sounded like a scared and gentle child. To kill one of these timid men and take the treasures they valued most seemed cruel. Why would her father kill a monk who was unarmed and peaceful? She felt a flame of anger burn inside her, partly that her father had been so brutal, but also that he was not here for her to argue with. Yet now he was trying to send her a message. He was trying to lead her to treasure . . . It was all too much for her mind to unravel. So she did as her uncle asked and put the parchment, tablet, and bone fragment into a bag.

Running to the back of the room, she found her mother cradling her sleeping brother.

'He cried himself to sleep,' Brianna said. 'He was sorry to have broken the wolf. I think we all saw it as a last little bit of your father's love here in our home. I heard the Jarl's men at the door. What did they want?'

'They came for Magnus. Some new saga is unfolding at the hall and uncle wants me and Fen to join him there,' Alva replied. 'He said I must leave this bag here with you. Will you keep it safe?'

She passed it to her mother, but as their hands met Brianna grabbed Alva's wrist, pulling it towards her. Looking deeply into her daughter's eyes, she said, 'Alva, you are being drawn into the plots of men—powerful men. We women are powerful, but we are kept apart from so much of the world, which men more freely explore. They have done things and seen things we have not, and I worry for you, that your gentle spirit will be changed by their world.'

Alva paused for a moment then slowly peeled her arm away. Her emotions were rushing like waves, crashing one on top of the other, and she worried that kind words from her mother might bring them flooding out in a deluge of tears.

Brianna continued: 'Before your father left, we exchanged strong words. He was worried that I was too protective of you. He has always been the one to put a sword in your hand, or lead you towards danger in the mountains. I love you and Ivan so very much, and with every winter that you grow I fear more for your safety. I know I keep you here in the home more than Bjorn liked, but his path for you leads to danger, while mine keeps you safe. And Magnus being here with us simply made you more hungry for adventure. I only want to protect you.'

Standing up as strong and as tall as she could manage, her outline picked out in the light of the doorway, Alva spoke softly. 'I feel the spirit of Lagertha and all the shield maidens burning in me. I'm not content to stay at home, play mother, and tend to the men. I want to know more of the world, and all the men and women in it. I wish you could believe in me more, mother. I know you fear for me, but I cannot change what I am. I need to investigate—it's like a hunger inside me. Uncle and Father both see this in me, and I would love for you to see it too. I know this will hurt you, but right now I need to go.' She pulled her hand away gently.

Calling for Fenrir, who had been sleeping by the bed, Alva bent down on her knees and held his muzzle.

'Fen, Mother fears for me, but we have to help Uncle. Do you swear to protect me?' He looked with baleful eyes at Brianna, then stood upright, close to Alva's leg.

'Alva,' her mother said, 'I have always known you have a shield maiden inside you. It's your father's fault, from all those days spent pouring tales of battle and adventure in your ears. I know you are strong. But others can be stronger and more brutal. I don't want you to go out tonight.'

Alva turned towards her mother once more. 'I have to,' she said. 'If you knew more about what we seek, you'd understand.' With a stronger stride than she felt in her heart, she moved towards the door and out into the town. Her heart, however, felt the tie with her mother being stretched with every step.

The afternoon was drawing in, and at this time

of year the days were short. It would be dark soon. Alva pulled her cloak tight around her, and Fenrir bounded alongside her, feeling the wind in his fur. They saw that the doors of Jarl Erik's hall were wide open as they approached, and Alva could hear angry voices inside.

'We have a right to the treasure if we are the ones who find it,' one voice echoed. The speaker had a different accent, from further south, and Alva didn't recognize him. He sounded young and boastful. 'The monk and English warrior passed through our town two days ago and they could not stop their whispers of treasure. They wanted us to read their runes and help them translate, but they were foolish. We told Jarl Gudmund that we had knowledge of great treasure here in Kilsgard and he gave us permission to find it and claim it for him and for our people.'

Jarl Erik's voice rose up above the clamour, loud and strong. 'Younglings, you have barely a beard hair between you, and yet you think you can enter our town and stride into a mystery that we ourselves are still battling to unravel? Be wary. This is not a simple story of buried treasures and gold lust. There are strange and dark strands being woven by the Norns. Two men have gone

missing. Someone or something is picking off those that search for this treasure. We are trying to understand it, but at this moment we are—I'm not afraid to say—terrified at what is assailing our town. I urge you to return to your homes and abandon this foolhardy venture.'

Alva saw a short, skinny youth, his dark hair falling in wispy strands around his smooth face. He spoke in a high-pitched, petulant voice. 'Old man, you and your men clearly do not have the courage or the strength to find this treasure. When the monk stayed in our town we had time to examine the carved casket. We know what the runes said, and we know where we have to go. But out of respect for your land, Jarl Erik, we have come to inform you that we will be taking possession of the items we find.'

Jarl Erik spoke up—'You must tell us what they said,'—but at that moment the three visitors turned on their heels and, smirking, swept out through the great doors of the hall. Alva examined them closely as they passed her. They must have seen barely fifteen winters each and were covered in silver—an outward sign of great wealth. She thought they looked like silly, rich boys. Giant's Finger would swallow them up. As she watched, they mounted their horses outside the hall, whose hooves roused a cloud of dirt and debris. The party disappeared into the fading winter light, their eyes set on the mountain.

Magnus ran out of the hall after the two men, almost crashing into Alva in his haste. 'This is bad,' he said anxiously. 'No one should be on this trail until we know more of where the missing men have gone. We simply don't know enough yet. While we have started to decipher the clues, we are nowhere nearer to knowing where Bjorn hid the bones. These foolish boys cannot know any more than us, so, like the Englishmen before them, I fear they will find themselves in great danger on the mountain. There is someone out there who is attacking those who seek to find the treasure.'

'Why don't you send Hraf after them?' Alva asked, spying the black bird on Magnus's shoulder.

'Good idea,' he replied. 'The bird can be my eyes—watch them, and let us know if anything happens.' Taking the raven on his hand, he looked closely into its eyes and began muttering and gesturing towards Giant's Finger. Alva leant with Fen against the entrance to the hall, listening again to what was unfolding.

It was busy inside Meginsalr. Men were shouting and slamming drinking vessels on oaken tables. Some were arguing with the Jarl that they were being cowardly and should search for the treasure themselves. Others wanted to know what information the Jarl had about the location of the treasure. Why should Magnus be investigating, and if he was first to find it, wouldn't he simply take the treasure for himself? They argued for some time, while Alva listened, whittling sticks with her knife in case anyone thought she was eavesdropping.

Once Hraf was sent on his way, a black speck in the winter sky, Magnus turned to Alva.

'Uncle,' Alva said, 'they really hate us in the hall right now. The men are impatient for treasure, and they think by doing our own investigations we are trying to steal it from under their noses. Their pride is hurt by these young adventurers, and they want answers.'

'I know, Alva. We have work to do. Come with me, and bring Fen,' he said, taking her by the shoulder and moving her from her safe space by the entrance, back through the doors of the hall.

Alva did not want to go further into this throng of angry Vikings and their nest of serpentine, slippery words, but a hush fell as they approached the burning fire in the centre of the room. She felt strangely safe with her uncle's hand gently guiding her.

There were about twenty broad, bearded, and brutal-looking men arranged on the benches around the sides. Jarl Erik strode towards Magnus and drew them closer to the hearth. Fen gave a little growl. The men shot wary glances at the wolf as he trotted along behind Alva.

'Thank the gods that you have returned, Magnus,' the Jarl said. 'The men are full of questions, and you are the only person who can answer them. Tell us, do we know who has taken the monk and the English warrior? Do we know what this treasure is and where it is hidden?'

Magnus drew himself up and cast a hard look around the room. After what seemed like a long pause, he spoke calmly. 'Good men of Kilsgard. This past day and night have been full of complexity. Two men have vanished, and along with them a casket covered in runes. It claims to lead the reader to a hidden hoard. I am still trying to unravel exactly what this treasure might be, but can only know for sure when I have fully decoded the messages carved into the casket. Once I do so you will all have the truth, but until then, the more you know, the more chaotic our search will become.

'This is my niece, Alva. As many of you know, she is a keen investigator and can seek clues and unpick riddles like no other in Kilsgard.'

Alva tried to make herself disappear under the steely looks of the men in the hall by shrinking behind the hearth. Yet she was surprised by her uncle's praise. He'd never said these things to her.

'Together we have been working through evidence discovered on the mountain and here in the hut where the monk was taken. We have found clues that may lead us to the treasure, but as yet there is no explanation for who is taking men in the night. The identity of this foe is still a mystery, and while it remains so we must be cautious. There is a violent soul wandering through Kilsgard.'

He stopped abruptly, as a loud interruption echoed from the back of the hall.

'Cautious!' came the deep, croaking voice. Sigrunn slid into view from the gloom as if she was floating across the floor. Alva felt her blood run cold as the seer moved closer to them. 'You are telling strong Viking men to be cautious? It is not a mystery as to why our town is so embroiled in turmoil. It is Loki. The god is toying with us. He dangles the promise of great wealth, but he hides it amidst chaos. His message is clear. He demands our gifts, and we must move forward with the sacrifice. This is something we must do without hesitation.'

Fenrir growled quietly as the ghoulish woman drew closer, her joints clicking with every step.

'I will accept no more delays, Erik. We must conduct the sacrifice once darkness has settled. We should start the preparations right away.'

Alva, feeling sick to her stomach with nerves, edged towards the crone and spoke very quietly. 'We are in the middle of an investigation, venerable Sigrunn.'

Turning her icy stare on Alva, the seer parted her cracked lips in a sinister smile. 'Was that you who spoke, young Alva?'

She nodded slightly.

'Ah youngling,' the old woman continued, scratching the wiry white hairs on her chin, 'you should not be so reckless. Particularly as

you have seen your own death so recently. You dreamt that danger was waiting for you on Giant's Finger, yet you follow in the footsteps of an ageing man, your uncle, in his tedious investigations. Have you not the heart of a shield maiden? Are you not driven to act? To appeal to the gods for strength?'

She drew even closer to Alva, and pointed a disfigured finger towards her.

'You need the protection of the gods even more than most, youngling Alva. You are marked by the Norns. I can feel it on you. I can almost see their web wound around you.'

As Alva looked around the hall the men were nodding their heads in agreement. She was burning with rage and hatred for the bitter old crone who hovered so close to her face, yet she was also quivering with fear. Sigrunn terrified her.

Jarl Erik raised his voice. 'So say you and all the gods. The sacrifice will take place upon darkness.'

Sigrunn smiled, showing her cracked yellow teeth. Shifting her unblinking gaze from Alva, and with an air of triumph, she turned to sweep from the hall. Alva shuddered as she felt the cold chill Sigrunn had brought with her slide away.

Her uncle rounded on the Jarl. 'This is the most useless thing we can do right now. We need time. Alva and I are getting close to understanding the runes. To whip the town up into a frenzy of ceremony and sacrifice tonight is dangerous, particularly as there are now three strangers wandering on Giant's Finger, as well as a potential murderer.'

But as he spoke, his words were drowned out by boos as the men of the hall took to their feet. Jarl Erik grabbed Magnus by the arm and steered him towards the door. Alva followed with Fenrir, looking over her shoulder anxiously. 'You are unpopular with the men right now,' the Jarl whispered. 'They think you are hiding runic secrets from them, and they envy the liberties I have given you. Play along with the ceremony. Show you want the chaos to stop. Bring your sheep for slaughter, and we can try to settle the anxieties that are flowing through Kilsgard.'

They had reached the door, with Fen growling threateningly all the way. Some of the men were following them, and, sensing the rise in tension, Magnus took Alva by the wrist. 'Come on girl,' he said. 'Let's leave this madness for now. It will only increase as the night grows older.'

***

Back at their hut, and with a storm brewing in his eyes, Magnus smashed through the doors angrily. Ivan gasped, and let out another huge howl.

'Oh thank you, Magnus,' Brianna exclaimed. 'I've only just settled him from his last attack of screaming!' Alva, still burning with a rage of her own, slammed herself down onto the bench and reached for a cup of ale, trying to calm her racing heart.

'The insanity of these people!' Magnus bellowed, landing himself on a seat and banging his fists on the table. 'They persist in their crazy rituals, and ignore reason.'

'What are you talking about?' Brianna asked, sweeping up the whimpering Ivan and sitting next to Magnus.

'They want a sacrifice,' Magnus replied, 'and they want it now. Apparently that will fix the drama that is enfolding our town, and bring the lost Englishmen back. It is folly. And we . . . we have to present our sheep for slaughter.'

Alva had heard the Jarl make this statement, but the reality of it slowly dawned on her. They only had a few chickens and two sheep to provide them with eggs and wool. Alva was very fond of both sheep, and she had named them Saemr and Heppinn, 'soft' and 'happy'. They were part of the family, sleeping in the hut during the cold winter months. She could not bear to see one of them beneath Sigrunn's knife.

Alva rounded on the room. 'I am not letting that old crone have our sheep. She can't have them! We have to find an answer to this before the ceremony takes place. I think we should look at the inscriptions again and see if we can find any more clues that could help us solve this, before Sigrunn begins her bloodbath.

'Mother,' she said, 'I'm sorry we have told you so little of what's been taking place in Kilsgard, and what mysteries Uncle and I have been unravelling. I know you are angry with me, but we need your help. Do you still have the bag I gave you?' Slowly, Brianna went to the family chest, and unlocked it with the large metal key she wore around her waist. This chest had always intrigued Alva. It was where her mother kept the most precious things their family owned, but Alva had rarely been allowed to look inside it. Brianna drew the bag out, and Alva laid the documents out across the table in front of her.

Brianna's eyes widened in amazement. 'Parchment,' she said. 'I have not seen so many of these documents since I left my Irish homelands. Why are these here in Kilsgard?'

'One of the men taken in the night was a monk from Lindisfarne,' Alva replied. 'We found them in his bag, although he himself had been seized in the night. He left other clues too—runes that he scratched onto the wall. Runes that I think were part of a message for us from father.'

Brianna's pale Celtic skin became even more washed out as she quietly digested Magnus's words. After what seemed an age she said, 'you think this has something to do with Bjorn?'

'Yes, mother. Uncle has told me of their journey to the English isle of Lindisfarne, and how he and father brought back some Christian treasures.'

'Relics, Brianna. The bones of saints,' Magnus cut in. 'From your early life as a Christian in Ireland, you must know of relics and their value.'

'I do,' she said, still looking startled, 'and I know Bjorn did too. Is that what you and he argued about upon his return? Bjorn should have told me of this.'

'I think he would have, Brianna,' Magnus replied, 'but the opportunity to go a-Viking came up and he left so suddenly. I think Bjorn carved the runes onto the casket when he realized he was the only one who knew the whereabouts of the bones, hoping that the three of us would work together to decode it. I don't think he meant to be away for long, and he must have intended the casket to reach us.'

Alva spoke slowly and deliberately. 'But his journey has gone on for much longer, and now the casket has fallen into someone else's hands. Through the twists of the Fates we have a chance to decode his message now. I think we have to work together if we are to understand father's message. That was what he meant when he said we would find "riches of the heart and soul"—I think this casket is a way of giving us treasure that could make us rich, but also a way to bring us closer together.'

Brianna took a deep breath. 'My darling girl, you did not know me before I became a clucking mother hen. In Ireland, I was the daughter of a king, and a powerful princess. I had an eager mind and the strength to outwit any man. I was much like you. Motherhood has tamed me and made me fear for my family, but I will show you tonight that I can be every bit the shield maiden you are. How can I help you both?'

Excitedly, Magnus shuffled the objects on the table, pulling out the tablet and stylus from his pouch. 'You can help us make sense of these documents, Brianna. We have already made some progress, so let's see what we have.'

Alva, relishing her mother's attention, butted in. 'The monk's scribbles tell us he met with Vikings in Francia. From that point he sets out on a journey north towards Kilsgard. We know from the strangers in the hall that he stopped at a nearby town in search of someone to help him read the runes. His carvings on the wall of Jarl Erik's hut suggest that he had committed much of the casket's symbols to memory. We also know that the treasure he sought was connected to Lindisfarne and their saints. But mother, we need your help with the runes. We have to come up with a complete translation, so that we can search for the treasure. It may lead us to the missing Englishman, we need to do this to help all of Kilsgard out of this spiral of madness.'

Taking Alva's hand, Brianna looked into her

eyes and smiled tenderly. 'If these runes are from your father then this is our quest. We will do this together.'

They worked away at the tablet, passing it between themselves, and debating exact words for certain encoded runes. Alva knew she and Magnus had already decoded most of them, but she enjoyed watching her mother's quick mind figuring them out for herself.

Darkness was creeping around the edges of their home, so Brianna stood and lit a candle, bringing it to the table. Magnus placed his tablet down. 'This is what the casket may have said: "For treasures of the gods, journey to Kilsgard. Joys of Western foes lie hidden in a dark place at the birch tree. From Jarl Erik's hall, journey to Giant's Finger. Follow . . ." The monk's carving halted mid-sentence. I wonder if this was because he was disturbed? It's so frustrating!'

'We can learn a little from this however,' Brianna said. 'We know that we have to find a dark place near a birch tree—it could mean a shady spot, or even some sort of cave.

'The trail begins with the mountain,' said Alva. 'But what about the lid? It says our names over and over again, but perhaps we missed something.'

She drew the piece of bone towards her, running her fingertips over the symbols. The sequence of repeating symbols were surrounded by lightly carved beasts that writhed into one another, biting onto each other's limbs and bodies. Her father had clearly taken great care with crafting the box.

ᚠᚢᛚ ᛗᚦ ᛊᛟᚷ

'These are our names,' Alva said, 'But look on this second row, there is another symbol carved next to my name here. I hadn't seen it properly before, as it's carved smaller and lighter than the other runes.'

Magnus held the bone fragment up to his eyes. 'So, Alva, here you have the two runes for your name, and laguz ᛚ. What does that rune mean?'

'It means "lake", uncle,' she replied, and suddenly Alva felt a cold chill run down her spine. 'My lake,' she said quietly. 'The lake where father used to take me. That's where he wants us to go.' She looked up excitedly at her mother. 'He took me there on his last day in Kilsgard.'

Magnus's eyes widened in realization. 'He has chosen a place that only we know of. This is his final part of the riddle. Only we can find the treasure, because only we know the landmark he has encoded here. Perhaps he has left further clues at your lake.'

Silence fell. Alva sat stunned. They had decoded these runes. They had found a clear trail. They had heard her father's voice through these symbols, and could now travel where he was guiding them. But before they could discuss how and when they might follow this trail, the sound of a gong rang through Kilsgard.

It was time for the sacrifice.

Stones from the Sky

Brianna stood, went to the front of the hut and opened a shutter. Darkness had engulfed Kilsgard, as had a layer of bright snow. The air had a biting chill, which crept into the warmth of their home and nibbled at their cheeks. Brianna said reluctantly, 'We have to go.'

Magnus stood up angrily. 'This is superstition and nonsense. The gods are not responsible for the missing men. There is someone else in these mountains who seeks Bjorn's treasure. He is roaming around our town, picking off men, and we need to find him before he takes anyone else.'

'No, Magnus,' Brianna said, turning her cold, green eyes on him. 'We have to follow what the village wants. If they demand sacrifice, we cannot be the only ones who refuse. We have to take Heppinn with us. Otherwise we will be excluded by all of Kilsgard. I live alongside these people. I'm already an outsider, brought here from a distant land. If I refuse to take part in the rituals it will be impossible for me and Alva to remain in this community. We have to leave for the ceremony right away.'

'But, Mother, we have to get to the lake and follow Father's trail,' Alva whimpered. 'Why can't we go straight there?'

'No, Alva,' her mother replied curtly. 'Sometimes we can be led by our hearts, and sometimes we must be led by our heads. We must honour tradition, but if you really feel this needs solving urgently then we can go straight to the mountain from the sacrifice.'

She grabbed her thick cloak from the bench and swung it over her shoulders. It was beautiful, covering her completely to her feet. Father had brought it back from one of his journeys. It was a deep red, woven with metal threads in the shape of birds. When she moved towards the door, the lamplight illuminated the outlines of their wings, and they seemed to fly gracefully over the red cloth.

Alva put on her cloak. It too was a gift from

her father, but it was less ornate than her mother's. It was made of thick dark wool, and around the shoulders was a collar of fur. She had been told that the wolf whose fur now kept her from the cold had tried to attack her father as he had been travelling in the far north. Beneath the green lights that had danced across the sky that evening, her father had killed the creature. He'd told Alva that because the cloak was made beneath the Northern Lights it had magic deep within it—that the cloak would always protect her.

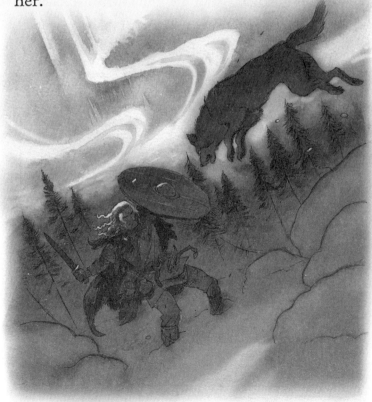

Magnus hesitated, but reluctantly swung on his cloak too. Brianna bundled Ivan into some furs, Alva grabbed Fenrir by the scruff of his neck, and they left their warm sanctuary, stepping into an eerie, snow-covered Kilsgard. Heppinn was in the pen outside, nestling her nose into her sister's wool to keep warm. Alva felt tears prickle behind her eyes as her mother placed a rope around the sheep's neck and pulled her away from her sibling. Their neighbours were in their yard too, chasing a chicken into a corner, and attempting to get it into a basket. The sound of anxious animals filled the streets and on the main path people were moving towards the brightly lit hall. Fenrir was agitated as he walked alongside Alva and she kept one hand on his back at all times to stop him rushing at the other animals.

They got in step, dragging a black-eyed Heppinn reluctantly behind them. The crowd were thrumming with a mixture of anxiety and excitement. One of Alva's friends, Leif, came running over.

'Isn't this brilliant, Alva?' he said.

'Not really,' she replied. 'We have to take Heppinn to be slaughtered! Which of your animals are you bringing?'

'We're taking one of the goats,' Leif replied casually. His family had a larger plot with more animals than her family. Leif always had the sturdiest shoes, the best belt fittings and more plentiful food than most of the other children. Alva wasn't surprised that he didn't care about their goat.

'I think the sacrifice is going to be pretty gruesome,' said Leif, a glint in his eyes. 'I hope I can get a good spot near the front. I want to see it all.'

Alva gave him a disgusted look as they arrived at the main clearing in front of the hall. Stalls were set up around the edges, selling warm drinks, beer, and delicious-smelling food. Torches illuminated the large space and in the centre a wooden platform had been constructed. It was empty, save for a huge metal bowl and a stool. On top of the stool, Alva could see the blade of a long, sharp knife, flickering in the light. Brianna grabbed her arm and whispered into her ear, 'Don't leave my side tonight. I want to know where you are, so no wandering off.'

Alva didn't want to wander off. The evening had a terrible thrill about it. Snow covered everything and the villagers looked unrecognisable, their faces covered with hoods or scarfs. Ivan ran to a nearby stall, grabbing at the baskets in search of sweet-smelling treats. As Magnus pulled him back, two figures approached. In the light of the torches, Alva could see it was the old ironsmith, Ingmar, and his wife Elin. As Ivan escaped Magnus's clutches, Alva moved towards her uncle, and their conversation drifted over.

'. . . but what if he comes to one of our houses?' Elin was asking. 'And I don't understand how he was able to take the monk from under the Jarl's nose. Maybe it's supernatural.'

'Don't be foolish, wife,' Ingmar said. 'There is a man, or maybe more than one man, that is behind these abductions. Magnus, I and some of the other villagers are frustrated at doing nothing. We want to head into the mountain with our weapons and hunt down this villain. Do you know where he might be hiding?'

'We are getting closer, but his location remains a mystery,' Magnus replied. 'I need to speak with the Jarl, but first we have to get through this performance. I am concerned, too, that those reckless young men went onto the mountain alone. I've sent my raven to follow them, but I am worried about anyone venturing into the mountain in the dark. If we go, we need to be careful and coordinated. We must not get wrapped up in bloodlust and passion.'

Alva stopped listening to her uncle at that point, because a word carried over from another conversation and caught her attention. She heard her father's name, and realized her mother was talking to her oldest friend, Gudrun. She had sidled up and was whispering nervously. Alva had known Gudrun and her husband Ingeld since she was a baby. As they had no children of their own, they had often spoilt Alva and Ivan with toys and treats. Ingeld was one of the townsmen still away a-Viking with her father, which might explain why Gudrun looked so sad, thin, and anxious tonight.

The two women had their heads pressed together, and were speaking quietly amidst the noisy throng of people. Listening carefully, Alva heard that Gudrun was questioning her mother on what had been happening.

'Any news of Bjorn? And what are Jarl Erik and his men going to do about these missing men? Surely they will head into the mountains to find out who took the Englishmen?' Alva thought she seemed rather breathless and agitated.

Their conversation halted abruptly as another loud gong rang out around the clearing. Jarl Erik strode out of the hall in his finest furs and jewels. On his head he wore a ring of birch-leaves, the tree sacred to Loki. Behind him came two of his karls, carrying a huge wooden statue of the god. The face was carved with deep eyes and a curling moustache, which followed the outline of a smiling mouth. Alva found the statue unsettling, as if the god was sneering at her.

Women dressed in long dark gowns followed Jarl Erik, beating a steady rhythm on calfskin drums. Once the Jarl and his procession had reached the platform, everything went silent. More snow began falling slightly faster as a biting breeze swept across the people of Kilsgard. Another gong sounded and Sigrunn slinked out from the hall. She was dressed in white, her head covered with a hood. She carried a flaming torch in front of her as she moved, ghost-like, towards the people. In the centre of the clearing, a huge bonfire had been constructed, ready to cook the meat from the unfortunate animals, for the feast that would follow the sacrifice. Sigrunn moved towards the pile of logs and bent her torch to light it.

Another gust of ice-cold wind, this time stronger, rushed between the gathered people. Sigrunn suddenly dropped the torch and it hissed as its flame went out in the snow beneath her feet. A gasp went around the crowd. Magnus turned to Alva and whispered, 'I'm sure the old crone knows that is a bad omen.' Alva laughed—nervously and far too loudly.

Sigrunn turned towards them, her eyes settling on Alva. 'You laugh, child? Well, if it's so funny, you shall bring me the next torch. You are already marked by the Norns, after all. Fetch me a flame.'

Alva felt her heart racing and hesitated for a moment, but Brianna pushed her gently forward, and she walked slowly towards the hall. Feeling the eyes of all the bystanders burning into the back of her head, Alva reached up to the brackets on the side of the building and took down one of the flaming torches held there. She lifted it towards Sigrunn, but as she did so the crone cackled, so loudly it echoed around the clearing.

'No. Now you must light the fire. You can

begin our ceremony. If the flame extinguishes for you too it is an omen. You are cursed by the gods.' She sneered the final word, and bowed in a mock gesture of reverence.

Looking around the circle of expectant faces, Alva steeled herself, swallowed hard, then threw the torch into the heart of the bonfire. She held her breath, watching for flickering flames. It felt like an eternity and silence gripped even the noisy, anxious animals. Then, with a roar, the heart of the fire came to life. Alva felt relief warm her as the flames spread upwards. Sigrunn mocked a bow at her, then slid up towards the platform to stand alongside the Jarl.

Alva scurried back to her mother, and Brianna whispered in her ear, 'That was a test. And you passed!'

The snow was falling fast and thick now. The wind was churning the fire into a frenzy.

'People of Kilsgard,' Sigrunn began in a loud voice. It grated down Alva's spine. 'We are here today because we find ourselves in need. We are beset with strange events. Men have been taken; one from the mountain, and one from our own Jarl's hall. There is mischief and mayhem creeping through our town, and it is the desire of the great god Loki that we feel his hand at work. We have displeased him. I fear he is disgruntled that our men who went a-Viking in spring have not returned to us as promised. He requires a sacrifice so we can show him that Kilsgard is still loyal to all the gods. Have you brought your sacrifices?'

She opened her brittle arms wide, and the crowd murmured a collective 'yes'.

'Good,' she said through a menacing smile. 'We must together ask Loki to come here to us. We will call for him with our chanting, and when we feel his presence, we will offer him our gifts.'

The women began to pound on their drums again, as Sigrunn set up a low and haunting chant. Around her, Alva heard others strike up the chant: 'Loki, you are welcome. Come to us.' As more joined in, the air became colder still. The snow slowed for a moment, then in the distance a rumble of thunder crashed, from the heart of Giant's Finger.

A lady next to Alva turned wide eyes towards her. 'Do you think it's Thor? Is he displeased we call on his rebellious brother, Loki?' Alva shifted uncomfortably foot to foot, anxiously looking towards the clamourous skies.

The thunder had shaken the crowd, but still Sigrunn persisted with her chant. There was more thunder, and Sigrunn raised her voice above the sound. 'The gods can hear us. Loki is coming! We must begin the sacrifice. Bring forward your offerings.'

Brianna tightened her grip on Heppinn's rope and began leading the terrified animal towards the platform. Alva felt desperation rising inside her as the sheep looked around at the crowd, cowering next to Sigrunn on the platform. She couldn't stand to watch this happen. Fenrir growled loudly beside her.

With a flash of shining metal, Sigrunn lifted the knife, and called, 'Loki, receive our offerings, and bring peace back to Kilsgard!' The thunder rang around the crowd again, this time louder and nearer. Then as Sigrunn reached towards Heppinn, two things happened. First, the heavens opened as a shower of hail crashed out of the sky. The hailstones were larger than Alva had ever seen. People called out in pain as they smashed down on the crowd. Secondly, a voice cried out from the sky. It was shrill, and it rose above the noisy chaos below: 'Gone!'

With an ear-piercing screech, Hraf was circling

above the crowds of Kilsgard, his black feathers all the darker against the white sky. He called out again in his semi-human voice, 'Gone!', then he swooped down to settle on Magnus's shoulder.

The villagers turned to look at Alva's uncle with suspicion and fear in their eyes. 'What does this mean?' one called out.

Magnus paused to stroke the raven. 'It's the three young men who went up into the mountain today. Something has happened to them.' The noise of the crowd grew, and their shouts were accompanied by the thud of heavy hailstones.

Sigrunn was hissing and murmuring under her breath, clearly confounded by the arrival of the bird and the message he bore. This was not a good omen and she knew it. With a screech, Sigrunn sank her eyes on Alva and Magnus. 'You have done this!' she hollered. 'You have brought shame on our sacrifice. You will feel the heavy hand of Loki on you now.' With a flourish of white material, she hastened from the platform and disappeared behind the crowd.

Jarl Erik moved to the front of the crowd and raised his voice over the clamour.

'The sacrifice shall be halted. A raven is always a messenger from the god Odin. We need to find out more about this news, and why the gods have allowed our ceremony to be disturbed in this way. I order you all to return peacefully to your homes. Magnus, myself, and the karls will go to the hall and discuss what should happen next.'

There were even more shouts of complaint at this, rising above the noise of the terrified animals being cajoled and moved. Magnus grabbed Alva by the hand and moved her towards to door of the hall. Fenrir followed attentively. Looking behind her, Alva could see Brianna heading home with Ivan tucked under one arm and Heppinn at the end of the rope.

The sound of the angry crowd was rising as Jarl Erik rounded on Magnus. 'You have created quite the drama tonight. That bird and its hideous words have halted the ceremony, and Sigrunn will be in a rage. You seem to have worked some wicked magic . . .'

'This is no magic,' Magnus broke in. 'The bird brings important news. If it tells the truth, then something has happened to the men who came to our hall earlier today. I sent Hraf to follow them, and now he tells me they are "gone". We have to investigate further.'

'Ha,' Erik laughed coldly. 'You and your investigations. And talking birds! There is a mad man raging through the town, taking people in the darkness, and you have given me nothing. I will not send my men out in this storm to search the dark slopes of the mountain on the words of a bird! No, Magnus. But we do need to do something. Myself and the karls will sit together and develop a plan to combat this threat. We need to investigate less, and actually do much more.'

'Well, I am going to listen to this bird,' Magnus said angrily, 'and find out what it knows about the young men. You sit here, drink mead, and talk with the karls. Declare your oaths and your boasts. I will continue to investigate, and I will follow the guidance of Odin's messenger, this raven, to find out what has happened.'

Magnus, Alva and Fenrir moved away from the hall. 'What are we going to do, Uncle?' she asked, once they were away from the main commotion.

'Alva,' he said, 'if Hraf says that the men are gone, I believe him. He has seen something in the woods, and he can take me there. This is too dangerous for you, but I need Fenrir with me if

I am to go into the mountain.'

'Wherever Fen goes, I go,' Alva answered stubbornly.

'Your mother will never allow me to take you into such danger,' Magnus answered.

'Tonight I am my father's daughter, but also my mother's. You heard her speak of shield maidens and strength. I don't care what dangers there are. Fen will not let anything happen to me, and together we can find more clues as to what is happening in Kilsgard. We can't wait. More lives might be lost.'

Magnus paused. 'Okay,' he answered finally. 'You can come, but you must not leave my side. If I give you an instruction at any point, you listen and act immediately. You keep Fenrir next to you at all times.'

Alva nodded in agreement and they began walking from the hall and along the path to Giant's Finger.

Brianna suddenly appeared beside them. She had been sheltering from the hailstorm under the canopy of one of the stalls and looked cold, worried, and flustered. Ivan was whimpering by her side, and the sheep was tugging on its rope. 'I have to take Ivan and Heppinn back home.

The hailstorm is getting heavier, and it is too chaotic here for a little boy.'

Magnus turned to her, 'I agree. But Brianna, I need to keep Alva and Fenrir with me. We will start to follow Bjorn's clues and go to the lake soon, but now we have something more pressing to investigate. If Hraf is right then more men have disappeared tonight. That means the kidnapper is still at large. I need Fenrir's skills to find them.'

Alva interrupted, stubbornly rounding on her mother, 'but as I told Uncle, where Fenrir goes, I go.'

A look of frustrated affection in her eyes, Brianna crouched towards Alva. 'Daughter, tonight I told you I want to help uncover the clues your father has sent us. I am sincere in that, but this is dangerous. It is your choice now. You can come home with me and your brother, to the safety of our home, or you can go to Giant's Finger with your uncle. I lay the decision at your feet.'

Flustered at these words, Alva replied slowly. 'Mother, I need to investigate. I need to. We can help the town tonight and make a difference. When we know more we will come back to you and begin following Father's riddle.'

With a sigh, Brianna straightened up. She locked eyes with Magnus. 'Look after her, on pain of your life.'

'I will,' he replied.

Brianna hustled Ivan and the sheep back down the busy street. Alva felt a pang of regret as her family moved away, towards the warm sanctuary of their home. But Fenrir nuzzled against her leg and with that she felt her determination crystallize.

Magnus had taken two lit torches from the hall and handed one to Alva as they set out. Hraf clacked his beak in Magnus's ear continuously. He seemed anxious to get going, and kept repeating the same word over and over, 'Gone. Gone.'

They began to move through the driving hailstones towards the mountain. Disgruntled, Fenrir bridled at the lumps of ice that pounded down on his back. He tried to tuck his nose under Alva's cloak as he trotted along, tying himself around her feet and blocking her way. So she could avoid the heavy stones flying down from the sky, she pulled the fur of her cloak up higher round her ears.

Magnus took the bird from his shoulder and

spoke quietly to it. Then Hraf soared upwards, and began to drift towards the mountain, leading the way.

'We know those foolish young men went up Giant's Finger. I would wager a band of silver that they made for the place where the English men camped. It's the only open clearing on the mountain side.'

Alva felt as if time had gone backwards as she retrod the steps she had made in the early hours of the morning, towards the clearing on the mountain. The ground was harder and more slippery than on her last journey, and on one occasion Alva missed her footing, landing heavily on the ice. Fen checked on her constantly, staying just a few strides ahead and not venturing off as he had done before. The wolf seemed to realize that there was even greater peril tonight.

As they climbed, the hail seemed to grow weaker, and in its place came flurries of snow. 'Well, at least that storm has passed for now,' Magnus called over his shoulder.

Hraf was spiralling above them, moving steadily forward, but ensuring that he didn't lose sight of them on the ground. His caws got louder as they approached the clearing, and finally he returned to Magnus's shoulder. 'Gone,' he croaked again in his master's ear.

The evidence was all around them. While Alva had strained to see the scuffs of feet a day earlier, the snow had now left a map in front of them. She could see that something dramatic had taken place here very recently. The men had built a fire and created a makeshift shelter out of branches and canvas. They must have tied their horses to a nearby tree, as hoofmarks were concentrated in that one place. But while it was clear the men had sat beneath the shelter, their footprints were not confined to that spot. Instead, the snow was churned up all around the still-smoking logs. It was difficult to see how many sets of feet had been there, as they all overlapped and crossed one another. What shocked Alva most, however, was the livid red blood that was splattered all around the clearing.

There was blood on the canvas, blood on the stones, and blood in trails running towards where the horses had been kept. It was a disturbing scene.

'This looks so different to the last time, uncle,' she said. 'It seems like there was a struggle again, but this is much more haphazard. The English warrior was kidnapped quietly. To me, it looked like he suffered a single blow, which knocked him out, then he was dragged to a horse and taken away. This looks much more violent and chaotic.'

'You're right, Alva,' Magnus replied. 'Your investigative skills are growing sharper by the moment. And something else is of interest to me. The men came with horses, yet there are no horses here now.'

'Perhaps the attacker took the horses too?' Alva suggested.

'Dragging three horses and three bodies down a mountain is no small feat. It seems to me that the men rode away from here themselves. I think they were harmed and frightened, but they managed to escape back to their home. They fought against their attacker, much blood was spilt, but they rode away from here—hopefully back to the kingdom of Jarl Gudmund.' Alva thought the clues certainly added up.

'Look,' she said, running past the trees. 'You can see that three sets of hooves have galloped through this snow, and the blood trails go with them.'

Alva got down on her knees to examine the disturbed ground. She felt across the snow, when her fingers settled on something smooth and shiny. She drew out a small object. 'Look, Uncle,' she said excitedly, holding it up. She was holding a broken piece of silver. 'It's part of a belt buckle, but it's broken. Where's the front part?'

'I think the front part has been taken,' Magnus replied. 'I can see a picture developing of what happened here. Do you recall, Alva, the three men were full of proud words when they left the hall? But when they got up here it must have been getting dark, and then the snow began. They sheltered together, until they were set upon by someone. The armed attacker then beat them and demanded their wealth.

'Do you remember how they were decked out like peacocks when they spoke to the Jarl? They were walking treasure-troves themselves. This broken belt buckle is what remains of a piece of silver that the thief has ferreted away for himself. Humiliated, robbed, and beaten, I think the men then escaped Kilsgard on their horses.'

'This does feel very different to the attacks on

the Englishmen,' Alva said again. 'Before it was the men that were stolen, rather than treasure.'

'You're right,' said her uncle. 'If we could find those young men's possessions, we could find the thief. There are so many riddles yet unanswered. It worries me that every person who has set out in search of Bjorn's treasure has been attacked and the closer we get to discovering its whereabouts, the more dangerous our investigation becomes.'

As they spoke, Fenrir had been sniffing around, close to the dying fire. He must be following a scent. Suddenly he let out a little whimper and ran over to Alva. A cut stretched across the front of his muzzle. The confused beast was now wrapping his pink tongue across his nose, frantically trying to lick the wound. 'What cut you, boy?' Alva asked, rubbing the wolf's face. She walked to where Fenrir had been, and bent down to examine. Under a cover of snow she could see something glinting in the moonlight. She pulled it free: a knife.

Magnus took it from her hand. 'Alva,' he said quietly, 'I know this knife. It is not a normal one. Look how wide it is. This is called a cleaver, and there is one man in Kilsgard who carries this with him everywhere.'

Alva realised that she recognized the cleaver, too. 'It belongs to the town butcher, Bjarke.'

'You have found a clue that ties this scene of carnage to one man. This is incredibly important.'

'Do you think it was Bjarke who attacked the men, Uncle?' she asked. 'If we want to understand what happened to the missing men, then surely we must return to the village and search Bjarke's hut. If we can find the men's missing silver then we have the answer as to who attacked the three young men here tonight.'

'I think you're right Alva,' Magnus replied. 'We will have to tread carefully, as the town is full of people tonight after the sacrifice. But we need to uncover more about Bjarke's involvement.'

'Well done, Fen,' Alva said, rubbing the wolf's nose as they raced back down the mountain. 'You found the most important clue! But, uncle, I know Bjarke. He is a bit of a fool and stuffs himself with ale but why would he come up here and attack these men? And what in the name of the gods could he know about my father, the casket, and the treasure? If we cannot fully decode the casket, how could Bjarke manage it? None of this is clear.'

They descended Giant's Finger with Fenrir trotting through the snow behind them. Speeding back towards Kilsgard, Magnus said, 'Alva, at this stage, all we can do is continue to follow the clues.'

The Safety of the Hall

The hall was still buzzing with activity as they returned, despite it being late and dark. While the karls sat inside, arguing over what they should do next, after the failed sacrifice the rest of the village had either gone home or decided to stay up drinking beer. Around the town, fires were burning and groups of men were singing, shouting, and spinning sagas. The atmosphere felt tense, and Alva feared that the men plying themselves with drink was surely not a good thing. Voices were raised through the streets, and she could hear proud boasts being proclaimed about who would capture the villain that was attacking their town.

'Uncle,' Alva said. 'I know we have to find out what has happened to the men, but what about father's treasure?'

'There is a threatening presence in our mountain,' her uncle replied, 'and people are disappearing, one after the other. If we can discover more about Bjarke's involvement in these latest attacks, then perhaps we can find out who else is on the trail of your father's treasure. We must know more about our enemy before we follow Bjorn's clues across Giant's Finger.'

'If we find the silver from the young men at Bjarke's hut, we know he was the one who attacked them tonight. Then we can find out if it is he who took the casket and seeks to decode the runes. You must remember that the English monk and warrior are still missing, and could be freezing on the side of the mountain somewhere. As well as your father's fortune, we must find them.'

'Well Bjarke's most likely in a tavern now, wrapping his massive mouth round a drinking horn,' Alva said. 'He's a terrible drunk, and is of simple mind. I imagine he would have put any treasures he stole from the men safely inside his hut before going drinking.'

'I agree,' replied Magnus. 'We must go to his hut and see if anyone is at home. Why don't you head back home for some sleep and leave Fenrir here with me?'

Alva glared up at her uncle through her matted fringe. 'Where Fen goes, I go,' she repeated. 'And I don't need to sleep.'

'I thought so,' answered Magnus grudgingly. 'You have your father's stubborn ways and thirst for adventure, Alva. Our investigations tonight remind me of when he and I used to explore together. To be honest, I'm very glad you're here with me.'

Bjarke's hut was to the east of the hall, on the opposite side of the settlement to their own. It grew quieter as they moved away from the throng in the heart of Kilsgard, and many of the huts were silent, as their inhabitants slept. The butcher's house faced onto the street, and during the day Bjarke set up a canvas stall out the front, where Alva had very often bought meat for the family's pot.

'We must listen carefully and find out if anyone is inside,' Magnus said, leaving the path and edging down the narrow space between Bjarke's hut and the leather-worker's next door. The shutters were closed and no lights shone from within. Magnus strained his ear to a crack in the wall. Alva held her breath, listening for the snores of the huge butcher. But there was nothing. Magnus pulled her back onto the street, where the main door to the wooden hut stood strong and, very clearly, locked.

'We can't get in,' Alva whispered. 'That is a strong lock, and Bjarke will have the key with him. The shutters are bolted, and I can see no other way in.'

'Well, let's see what I can do,' Magnus said, with a slight glint in his eye. He pulled his pouch open and began rummaging his hand deep inside. Alva could hear rustles, clinks, and clanks, as he riffled between his many useful treasures. Then he drew out a ring of metal. Around the edge were keys of all shapes and sizes. 'I had a key cutter in Helgö make this for me. He was a bit reluctant, but I persuaded him I needed it for my investigations. It doesn't open all locks, but includes most sizes and shapes of keys, and I've been lucky whenever I have used it so far.'

Despite her whole body ringing with nerves and excitement, Alva couldn't help but stifle a giggle in her thick fur collar. The contents of her uncle's bag never ceased to amaze her, and while she was shocked that he had such a collection of keys, she wasn't really surprised. She wondered what other locks he had been secretly opening.

He began placing each key into the lock in turn. It was a noisy business, and the metal rang out with each failed attempt. Alva kept looking around, fearful that someone would hear them. 'Don't worry,' her uncle said quietly. 'It means that no one is in, at least, and the neighbours will just think Bjarke is drunkenly struggling with his lock again.' At last, Magnus placed a large key with four teeth into the lock. After moving it back and forth, they heard the mechanism slide sideways. The door made an immense creaking noise, and opened.

The hut was completely dark, the fire was out, and the hearth was cold. Magnus brought his flaming torch inside and a warm light filled the room. Alva was startled by the mess inside. At one end, animal skins hung around the walls, while sections of beasts were either strung from the roof or laid out on the long table. The smell was hideous. The other side of the hearth was clearly Bjarke's living quarters. There was a straw mattress, with clothes and rugs strewn over it. All around the floor were tools, cooking utensils, shoes, cups and half-eaten food, and dirt covered everything.

'Bjarke has not looked after himself since he lost his wife,' Magnus said.

Alva recalled how the butcher had been married to a local girl, but she died giving birth. Neither mother nor child survived the ordeal. 'This place is disgusting,' she said, her nose covered to ward off the smell. 'How can he live like this?'

'Forget the mess, for now. We need to think where a man like Bjarke might hide stolen jewels and weapons,' Magnus said, casting his eyes around the room.

'Fen can help,' Alva said. 'If I let him smell that belt buckle we found in Giant's Finger, he should be able to find other objects with that smell on them.'

'Great idea! He really is a remarkable creature, Alva,' Magnus replied. 'You've trained him well.' Alva had spent many months experimenting with Fenrir's sense of smell. She had hidden objects around the town and enjoyed cajoling Fen as he sniffed the ground, following her footsteps, and eventually finding the hidden trophies.

Magnus drew the scrap of silver from his pouch and handed it to Alva, who held it under Fenrir's muzzle. 'Find,' she said clearly, looking the wolf in the eye as she spoke.

After a few seconds, Fenrir began moving around the hut, his nose close to the ground. He had to climb over all the debris that covered the floor and he moved bits of leather and scraps of material with his paws, searching for the scent. He paced from one corner of the building to the other, sweeping across from side to side. Eventually, he came back to Alva and stared up at her with dark, sad eyes.

'Don't worry, Fen,' she said, ruffling his fur. Turning to her uncle she said, 'It's not here. If Fen can't find it, it's not in the hut.'

Magnus rubbed his beard thoughtfully, tugging at one of the beads knotted carefully into the hairs. 'But what if it is in the back?' The yards of most of the houses in Kilsgard stretched out in strips of land behind them, and often owners would construct little outbuildings on this ground. They moved out of the house, locking the door as they left. Once again they squeezed through the narrow passage to the side, careful not to knock on the walls of the leather-smith's hut next door as they went.

The yard was as poorly looked after as the house. Weeds lay thick across the earth, and no planting or tilling had taken place for some time. Yet, as expected, a small, dilapidated hut reared out of the darkness at the end of the plot. Fen suddenly took off. He ran straight for the shack and began scratching at the wood.

The hut had a simple bar across the door, wedging it shut. Magnus heaved it open, and shone his torch inside. A rusty scythe hung on a hook, and dried-out bulbs, balls of tangled yarn, and planks of wood lay scattered over the floor. In the corner, however, was a bright piece of pale material. Fenrir made straight for it, and he pulled at the cloth with his claws. As the fabric fell back, the torchlight reflected back a heap of polished metal. Inside a wicker basket was a hoard of glinting weapons, silver bands, and fragments of jewellery.

'We've found it, Alva, the men's riches!' said Magnus. 'We've got him, but the jarl is not going to like this.'

Alva ruffled Fen's fur, proud of how well he had done, but inside she felt anxious. These investigations were a distraction from their main goal. They had to start following the runes. They already knew where to start—at her lake. Yet now they would have to show these treasures to the Jarl and question Bjarke. It would all take time and instead she wanted to decode the mystery laid for her by her father across Giant's Finger.

They left behind the dark squalor of Bjarke's house, Magnus dragging the basket of treasures with him through the snow.

Alva pondered what they had found as she trudged along the crisp white path. She couldn't understand how Bjarke fitted into the story. He was a drunk fool, but surely he hadn't the wits to kidnap two men and try to decode the riddle of the runes. What's more, if Bjarke had the Englishmen, where was he keeping them? They certainly weren't at his home. Something was missing. Something wasn't right.

They came to the main clearing outside the hall, which was still lit around the edges, as groups of men and women sat around fires under shelters, arguing and carousing. The huge bonfire in the centre still burned, but it was now pumping out plumes of black smoke against the white backdrop of snow-covered Kilsgard.

Magnus made for the door and banged his fist against it. One of the karls, Fleknir, opened the door. His eyes were bloodshot and he looked exhausted.

'It's you,' he murmured. 'You will not be welcome in here.'

'I will be when you hear how I have discovered more news of the night's events,' replied Magnus. 'Let me in.' He pushed himself past the karl, and Alva followed, leading Fenrir into the hall. The hall fell silent. Magnus walked straight to the central hearth, ignoring Jarl Erik. Alva moved alongside him, trying to keep her head held high while her instincts cried out to hide away in a corner of the hall, out of sight. In his loudest speech-making voice, he turned to the benches and began, 'Listen. A good deal has happened since I left you after the ceremony. You wanted to sit and talk, while I, a true son of Odin, wanted to explore and discover. With my niece, this wolf here, and my raven, we went to Giant's Finger on the trail of the three young strangers.' A call went up around the hall, but Jarl Erik silenced it with one finger.

'Be still,' he said. 'Magnus brings news, and I, for one, want to hear it.'

Magnus had the wind in his sails now, and was in full boast. 'You did nothing, while I used my mind's eye to search for information. My raven said the men were gone, and so they were. We made for the high clearing on the west side of Giant's Finger, where the monk and English earl had camped. There we found signs that a fierce struggle had taken place. There was much blood. Yet the three men and their horses had left the site, beaten, but, I think, still alive.

'Nevertheless, it was clear they had been attacked and their possessions had been stolen. We found broken belt fittings, which suggested they were robbed of their weapons. They were weak and young boys, but dripping in silver. A single strong man could deliver a beating and demand their riches. This is how it seemed to us. With the help of my niece and her remarkable wolf, we discovered this.' Magnus pulled the cleaver from his belt. 'We all know who it belongs to.'

'That's Bjarke's knife,' one of the men shouted out.

'Indeed it is,' said Magnus, turning on him. 'So we thought it very likely that Bjarke had taken the men's treasure in the night, and hidden it somewhere in his home. We travelled straight there—again doing something, while you men simply drank and talked. Bjarke was not there, so we explored his hut. We found nothing until the wolf Fenrir used his god-given gift of smell to lead us to an outbuilding. There the foolish butcher had hidden this . . .'

Magnus lifted the basket that he had dragged into the hall above his shoulders and tipped its contents onto the broad table in front of Jarl Erik. The sound of chinking metal rang around the hall as daggers, coins, and silver fittings poured across the wood. In the dancing flames of the burning fire, Viking eyes lit up with excitement. But then came sounds of shock and anger, ringing around the hall.

'How do we not know this is all down to you, Magnus?' said one of the men, from the shadows. 'This stinks of conspiracy. It is you who has had a bloodlust for the three men. You who trained your bird to disrupt the ceremony so you could run like a hero into the mountains and prove your wisdom to us. We have no witness to what you found. You could have put the cleaver there yourself.'

'I am a witness,' said Alva suddenly. Her voice was small, and cracked as she spoke. It felt hard to squeeze the words out of her mouth. She pulled back her wide fringe of hair, raised her head high and said again, 'I am a witness.'

The room hushed. Pausing, surprised by the silence, she tried to recreate the speech-giving voice she knew so well from the men of the hall.

'I swear by all the gods and goddesses. By Freyr and Freya, by Thor and Odin, that all my uncle says tonight is true.' Sweat dribbled down her back and her heart thundered inside her chest, but she carried on speaking. 'I have been with him every step, and I can testify to all he states. My wolf, Fenrir, found the knife in the snow. Look,' she said, pulling the beast forward and pointing to his nose, 'he cut his muzzle when he searched for it. And I can describe to you Bjarke's home, his yard, and the hut where we found the treasure.' Turning her eyes as confidently as she could manage towards the Jarl, she said finally, 'let Thor strike me down if I tell a word that is untrue.'

Magnus looked at her with an expression of gratitude, as she brushed her hair back over her face once again and pulled away from the hearth,

Fenrir shielding her as she went. 'But she is your blood relative,' another voice called up. 'She is sure to support you. And why should we listen to the words of a simple girl?'

Magnus took an angry step towards the man who had spoken, raising the butcher's cleaver towards him. Alva rushed to his side, pulling back his arm.

'Hush,' said Jarl Erik, standing up from his broad wooden stool and stepping forward. 'Calm yourself, Magnus, and do not raise weapons in my hall. Sit and put down that knife.'

Magnus reluctantly did as he was instructed.

'Now you have certainly been busy tonight,' Erik continued. 'As Jarl of Kilsgard I am not pleased when members of the town take justice into their own hands and fail to keep me abreast of what they are doing. But what you have found is of great interest.

'We all know that Bjarke has become more difficult and unhappy with each passing moon. If it is the case that you found his cleaver in the mountain, I, as Jarl, must discover the truth.' He turned to two of his karls. 'Tori, Grim, find Bjarke and bring him to the hall. He will be full of mead, and you know he is strong, so take weapons. Tell him I wish to see him immediately, but do not harm him.'

The two left the hall, grabbing their spears and shields from the entrance, where all the karls had to leave their weapons. No arms were allowed near the Jarl's hearth, so Uncle Magnus had created further drama by bringing the cleaver and stolen weapons to Jarl Erik's table.

'Magnus,' said the Jarl, 'you have displeased me in many ways today, but we are friends and I know you and the girl are wise at investigating. Come up to my bench and let me hear all the details you have. I will need to question Bjarke when he arrives.'

Servants entered the hall, bringing jugs of mead with them, and refilling the cups of the men around the benches, who kept their voices low. Anticipation hung heavy in the air. Magnus and Erik spoke quietly but energetically, while Alva and Fenrir slumped in a corner. Alva tried to warm her frozen feet, but the fire was some distance away.

The relative calm was shattered as the two karls reentered the hall, dragging an unsteady, dirty, dishevelled man between them. Alva sat up and paid close attention, cajoling her drooping eyelids into action as she leaned towards the new arrivals. She rose to her feet slowly.

'Bjarke!' Magnus's voice rang around the hall. The warriors lowered their cups, and stared at the group in the doorway. 'Bjarke!' her uncle boomed again, 'I found this basket hidden in your outbuilding. I have been to the mountain and seen where you attacked the young strangers. I have found your lost butcher's knife. Here, in front of the hall, I accuse you. You attacked the three younglings who came to our hall. You robbed them and took their wealth for yourself. Did you also attack the monk and the English earl? If so, where are you hiding them?'

Half man, half giant, the butcher planted his feet and slowly raised himself from where he'd hung between the two groaning karls. He was covered in grime, and his beard was matted with straw and flecks of food. He smelt even worse than his house, Alva thought, as he stumbled to his feet and moved towards Magnus with steady, heavy steps. Each time one of Bjarke's feet hit the ground she could sense the warriors of the hall shudder.

He stopped only a breath away from
Magnus, and lifted up his face, which was
covered with the scars of many battles. Bjarke
was old now, but Alva knew he had been
a-Viking with the strongest men of the town,
and had experienced the thrill of the fight.
His left eye was partly closed where the line
of an enemy's sword had cut across it many
years ago. His beard was still golden, but was
covered with the stain of mead. To Alva he
appeared fearsome, handsome, and huge.

'Is it me you speak to, great rat?' Bjarke hissed the words slurringly into Magnus's face. 'Has Loki climbed into your skin? What mischief do you make?'

'The whole town is full of terror at these night attacks, Bjarke.' Magnus replied, his voice quavering slightly. 'It is up to me to discover what is happening. My raven followed you today. You went to the hills, where the group of foolish, young treasure hunters were gathered together. Hraf told me the men were gone, and the mess you left at the site told me everything else. You stole the men's weapons—these weapons.'

Magnus lifted two silver daggers from the table. Other shiny objects had also tumbled out of the basket: glistening brooches, belt fittings, metal buttons, and many coins. Everyone in the hall eyed them greedily.

Bjarke drew his face even closer to Magnus's, breathing his words with a menacing grumble: 'Accuse me again, wretch, and I'll send you to Hel, with all the other sad, useless Vikings.'

Pulling himself up to his full height, Alva's uncle stared back. 'I found this at your home, hidden in your yard. You have taken these treasures from the poor young men, so is it you that took the Englishmen and the casket? Do you have your eye on a greater treasure still?'

Bjarke let out a huge, bellowing laugh. 'Stupid, ignorant fool!' Turning to the hall, he raised his voice so everyone could hear. He suddenly seemed sober and strong.

'I admit it—I stole from the pompous churls who came from Jarl Gudmund's lands. When they came into Kilsgard they passed by me, asking if I had heard talk of a great treasure. They were so rude and brash and boyish that I told them I had heard of a monk and earl, and a casket covered with clues. They wanted to know where the men were last seen, so I told them of the clearing in the trees on Giant's Finger.

'They were just three boys, with barely a beard hair on their chins between them. They were rich; covered in silver and armour. I knew they would camp there—so yes, I went for the easy pickings. They were so weak. The men struggled a little, but really it was like taking life from a lamb. I took their wealth, but I did not take the casket from the Englishmen. I have no interest in runes.'

'Why, Bjarke? Why did you steal from them?' It was Alva who was speaking now, moving towards the ranting man, and her gentle voice brought about a transformation in the giant.

Bjarke's huge shoulders slumped. He drew his bold gaze away from the hall and looked at his feet. 'I am poor,' he said quietly. 'Rest assured, I too want to know who is responsible for taking the other men, so they can taste the edge of my sword. I should not have gone to the young men, but I have nothing and they were so weak. I wanted their wealth for myself and knew I could take it. But I see that by doing this I created more terror for the people of our town . . . There is no honour in what I did. By the gods, I am sorry.'

He shrunk in on himself and the silent hall began to murmur. Magnus clasped him on the arm. 'I think you speak the truth,' he said to Bjarke. 'To make a speech in front of the hall is brave and I believe you. I felt that there were two different people responsible for these attacks, but this doesn't bring us any closer to knowing who has the casket. You have committed a crime, Bjarke. But judgement on this should come from the Jarl.' Turning to the men of the hall, he raised his voice, addressing them all. 'Now we have to work together if we are to cleanse our this threat which moves among us. We have to come up with a plan. Time is running out for the missing men.' Alva felt anticipation rising again, pushing away the tiredness that rang through her bones. She wanted to get moving. She wanted to crack her father's riddle. She wanted to get to Giant's Finger.

Shine a Light

Alva was tired. Deep-down exhausted. She sat huddled against one of the walls of the hall as the men talked on and on. Why did Viking men have to turn every speech into a boast or a saga? Fenrir had curled up by her legs and was keeping her feet warm with his thick fur. Her mind wandered as she listened to the endless oaths and arguments. This was ridiculous! They had the first location from the casket and could go there right away. All this talk and bluster was just delaying them.

Feeling Fenrir's gentle breath against her legs, Alva remembered how she had found him when she herself was only a girl. She had been running through the woods with a group of friends. Night was creeping in and the others wanted to go back to their homes, but Alva wanted one more adventure before bed. As darkness fell around them, the sounds of howls came from nearby. Her friends ran immediately, full of the fear their parents had poured into their ears about wolves baying for blood. But Alva wasn't scared. She walked towards the sound, not away from it. Beneath a huge pine tree she saw a single wolf, lying on its side. As she moved closer, the creature did not stir. Yet a small mewling sound was coming from it.

She came nearer and saw that the beast's leg was caught in a trap. The people of Kilsgard set up ropes and pulleys around the woods to trap deer for food, but this wolf had become tangled up some time ago. The wound around its leg was old and clotted. Still the beast didn't stir. It was dead. But as she turned to leave, she saw a small movement beneath the belly of the wolf. A tiny cub, still blind, was squealing up at her.

It was madness to approach. All around her the sound of howling was getting closer and any second now she could be attacked and bitten by razor-sharp canine teeth. But Alva felt so deeply for the sorry, pale, wriggling cub crying out for food and love. She couldn't leave it to die. So, quickly, she picked it up and tucked it inside her cloak, and ran back home.

It felt like the World Tree itself shook at the fury of her mother when she returned.

'A wild beast?' she ranted. 'It will bring the threat of the outdoors here within the sanctuary of our home. It will never be yours, Alva. It is from the forest, and it could kill any of us with a single snap of its jaw.'

But Alva's father remained quiet while her mother shouted to take the cub outside and leave it to the elements. Eventually he stood up and took the tiny thing up in his hands, holding it to the light.

'One of the sons of Loki, Fenrir, is a wolf. A wolf can be a god. If our little shield maiden can tame a wolf, will that not make her a god?'

He forbade Brianna from hurting the cub, and brought over a bowl of milk. Placing it on Alva's lap, he showed her how to use her finger to bring the feed to the starving baby wolf's pink mouth.

It lapped the milk up greedily, and as she sat there, cradling the cub, her father said, 'This wolf will protect you. He will be your guardian when I am not here. He will need to be fierce and strong when he grows up. He will need to be like Fenrir himself, the god-wolf. Name him Fenrir.'

And now Fenrir sat by her side. Alva could feel his chest steadily rising and falling as he slept. She loved him so much, and had shed so many tears into his fur, thinking about where her father might be. Her breathing joined his as she felt herself slipping towards sleep.

The noise of a copper cup rattling against the floor dragged Alva quickly back to waking. She didn't know who had thrown it, but several of the men were now standing and shouting, while her uncle was swinging his cloak dramatically over his shoulders.

'If you want to chase runes, so be it,' one karl was yelling at Magnus. 'We are warriors, and we will act like warriors. We will take a band of men, all the fighting men of the town, up into the mountains before sunrise. We will go door to door, gathering every able man of Kilsgard, and we will scour the land until we weed out this stranger and find the Englishmen. Then we will find the treasure.'

'You will ruin this,' Magnus replied fiercely. 'If you set a horde of angry men on the mountains, the criminal will make himself invisible. I think he knows the mountains well. When he hears you all clattering, shouting, and waving around torches he will bed down and we will never find him. We will lose the advantage we have. Right now we have a good idea where he is heading, and that is where we should go.'

'You go, fool,' came a shout from the benches. 'You go and chase your symbols, while we chase the criminal.'

'I will,' Magnus answered, swinging his cloak behind him and pulling Alva to her feet. 'Come on,' he whispered. 'There's no convincing men against their will. And these have iron for hearts.'

The bite of the cold night engulfed them as they left Meginsalr's warmth.

'If they are to spread like a loud, livid rash

across the mountain before dawn,' said her uncle, 'we have to follow our own clues as soon as possible, to try to find the answer to the riddle first.'

'We don't have all the runes,' Alva replied, wide awake now in the frozen air.

'But we have a very clear direction for the first location. The lid of the casket was a private message from your father to us, and we can follow his guidance. The difficulty is, because the runes include you, me, and your mother, I think she might be the only person who knows one of the destinations.' They looked at each other for a moment. They had many problems to solve before sunrise, but persuading her stubborn mother to join them on the slopes of Giant's Finger, in the death of night, was going to take all the wisdom of Odin.

Their hut was silent as they approached. The last few revellers had finally crawled to their beds, and the streets were empty. The sleeping residents of Kilsgard did not yet know that karls would be beating on their doors in the dark side of dawn, waking their children, terrifying their households, and demanding the men take up arms.

Inside the hut, it was still and dark. The fire gave off a little light, and Alva could see Brianna cuddling Ivan at the far end.

'We need to wake her,' Magnus said. He had a genuine look of fear in his eyes that she had hardly ever seen.

'I'll do it,' replied Alva, feeling determined. They had to solve the riddle from her father. She crawled close to her sleeping mother.

Brianna's red hair seemed to glow, and lay around her head like a fiery crown. She looked how Alva imagined the elf folk; ageless, luminous, and mysterious. But as Alva shook her gently by the shoulder, Brianna opened her piercing green eyes and at once was transformed into the formidable woman Alva was used to.

'Why have you woken me?' she asked quietly, brushing her hair back with long white hands.

'Mother,' Alva said, whispering so as not to wake Ivan, 'Uncle and I need to speak with you at once.' A look of anticipation crept across her mother's face as she gently placed Ivan flat on the mattress and stood up. Magnus was already sat at the table, and pouring himself a cup of ale from a jug. Two more full cups were already there, waiting for them.

Alva and Brianna sat next to Magnus on the bench. 'It has been a long night,' he said. 'We have all been awake for too long, and many in Kilsgard are ragged with tiredness. Their minds are not clear, and the Jarl himself is following poor guidance from drunk, exhausted men. He wants to find the stranger who took the Englishmen, before sunrise. They will wake the houses and launch a search across the mountain. It will be clumsy and foolish, since anyone hiding on the mountain will hear them and hide deeper.'

'Mother,' Alva said, 'you know that between us we have the answers to this mystery. Father sent us a set of directions. He wanted us three, and only us three, to understand the instructions on the casket. The lid referred to each of us by name. It must have been his strategy, that those closest to him would be needed if the treasure was to be found. And that only by working together, supporting each other, would we be able to solve the riddle. We know where my lake is, but I think this will lead us on to further locations that only we know of. We need you.'

Brianna took a slow sip from the cup and stood up, facing the fire. In this light, she looked like one of the gods, ready to determine the fates of men with one wave of her hand. They sat quietly, waiting for her to speak. Eventually she turned to them. 'I have watched tonight as you two take the trials of the whole town on your shoulders, plunging yourselves into danger, without a thought for our family.'

Alva shifted guiltily on the wooden bench, aware that she had been deceiving her mother throughout the past day.

'You've returned here, taken what you needed, and gone away again. You have left me and Ivan behind, without a thought for what would happen to us, or how we would feel if your adventures brought you to a bitter end.

'I understand what drives you. We are all fuelled with a fire and a desire for adventure— and your father, Alva, had it searing through his blood. But that need must be tempered by an understanding of blood-ties and the bonds that bind us. We have a responsibility to care for ourselves, so that those who care for us are not put through pain. I worry you don't have that care, Alva.'

Brianna sat back down next to her daughter and placed a thin pale hand on hers. 'I know I need to help you tonight. I too want to put an end to this, so that we can return to being a family. We will follow Bjorn's instructions together, and perhaps we can help the town tonight. Perhaps, also, it will bring us together again as a family, and rekindle the bonds that we have left untended for too long.' She sighed deeply, her speech finished.

Alva spent a moment turning her mother's words over in her mind. She had spoken nobly, and a deep sense of guilt gnawed through Alva's bones again. But above that feeling came one of warmth; a huge sense of gratitude and of admiration. Her mother had never seemed so strong and supportive as at that moment. Alva threw her arms around Brianna's neck, squeezing tightly. She whispered in her ear, 'I have wanted you by my side through everything. Tonight you will be.' They embraced, and Alva felt her mother hold on to the moment for as long as she could, before she finally released her.

'But I have some conditions,' Brianna said, standing again. 'Firstly, I will not let Alva be put in harm's way. There could be a violent criminal waiting for us at the end of these investigations, and how can we three defend ourselves? We must take weapons. I too know how to fight—

and I will do so for my daughter—but, Alva, I do not want you to fight.'

Alva and her uncle nodded their assent.

'Secondly, I won't put Ivan in harm's way either. He is only a baby. You must wait while I rouse Freydis and ask her to watch him. And finally, whatever the outcome of our search tonight, we must be in the Jarl's hands. If he tells us to stop, if he tells us to give him what we have found, or if he tells us we are breaking the laws, we bow our heads. Do you agree?'

Alva and Magnus exchanged a look. 'Yes,' they agreed. Brianna sprung into action. Things needed to be done. Ivan needed to be bundled in as many warm furs as she could find and trundled down the road to the kind crone two doors down. Bags needed to be packed with food and drink for the journey. Cloaks needed to be tied especially tight. The fire needed to be extinguished.

Eventually, Brianna stood in the door, tall, pale, and magnificent in her red cloak, with furs on her hands and a look of steely determination on her face. 'Let's go,' she said, and torches aloft, they stepped out together.

The night was transforming from dark black to a deep blue, as the threat of dawn crept around the edges of the mountain. They walked silently as they left the town, the snow helping to muffle their footfall. Once they were a good distance from the village gates, Magnus turned to them. 'We know the first part of the journey already, don't we, Alva? We have to head up towards the clearing and from there we can begin following Bjorn's directions. So you lead the way.'

Alva felt her cold, numb cheeks glow a little red at this, but she strode proudly to the front with Fenrir. He already knew where he was going, and bounded off ahead. Magnus had brought Hraf too and he sailed above them. Wolf and raven, their senses trained on the journey ahead—the beasts of battle were helping them.

As they moved up the mountain, Alva felt her mother draw closer.

'Alva,' she said quietly, 'I know you have done many things tonight. You and Magnus have not told me everything, but I am sure you have felt many different feelings throughout the night.'

'I have,' Alva replied. 'My mind is so full it could burst at the seams. But I have been feeling guilty, too. I wanted to help Uncle so much, but I've also known that a lot of what I've done would displease and hurt you.'

'At least you have felt it,' her mother replied. 'To do these things without feeling would make you cold. But I understand why you have, and I forgive you. I know that I have smothered you too much. You are approaching womanhood, and your father wanted so much freedom for you, while I feared it. Tonight we will set this right and we will channel the spirit of great shield maidens. We will find what your father wanted us to find. We are brave, we are quick, and we are clever.'

Alva smiled up at her mother, again feeling a rush of warmth spread through her. 'I am not afraid,' she said chuckling slightly. 'I am like the great Lagertha the poets sing of. She who had "the courage of a man and fought fearlessly". Tonight I will be fearless. And so will you. And so will Uncle.'

Brianna gave her daughter's arm a squeeze. 'I'm proud of you, Alva,' she said. But as Alva bathed in these comforting words, they heard a howl from Fenrir up ahead. They had arrived.

'This is the clearing where much of the drama has unfolded,' Alva said excitedly. 'Here, the English earl was taken—struck in the night and dragged away on a horse—and Bjarke attacked three men from out of town, robbing them of their riches.'

'Bjarke!' Brianna exclaimed. 'The butcher? Why would he do that?'

'Oh, we got to the heart of it,' Magnus answered. 'It was a simple case of a sitting duck and a greedy goose. He wanted their wealth and he was brutish enough to take it. But that was a distraction from what else happened here. The first attack is what we are interested in now. There was someone here who also knew of Bjorn's messages. Someone who had followed the monk and the earl on their journey to Kilsgard, and who wanted to stop them finding what is hidden in the mountain. It is he we both seek and avoid. We need to get to the treasure following our own directions, but it is very likely that our enemy is on the same journey. Our eyes and ears must be pricked like Fenrir's tonight. Now we have to go beyond this clearing and to the "lake"—Alva, show us the way.'

Pulling down her collar, she addressed her mother and uncle directly: 'There is a cove at the foot of this mountain, on the east side, that was precious to me and Father. If you follow me, I'll take you there. But watch where you tread.

It's pretty steep on this side.'

She wound behind the wall of rock at the back of the clearing and led them towards to the top of the slope, while Fen ran on ahead again. 'We need to get down this bank, to the river,' she said, taking her mother's hand. Together, carefully, they slid down the side of Giant's Finger. Reaching the bottom, Alva crouched by the water, and raised her torch.

'It's hard to see,' she said, 'but look at the ancient carvings. See that boat there?' She held the torch above the faint outline of a long ship. 'Father and I used to say that this ship brought the Jarl's ancestors to Kilsgard, and the giants to their doom. Can you see the other ship carved next to it? Father promised me that one day we would sail on a longboat together; with me at the prow, my hair whipping in the wind, on our way to adventures.'

Alva stood back from the riverbed and her mother drew close, wrapping an arm around her shoulder. 'I knew you and your father shared a special place,' she said quietly. 'That it was just for the two of you, and no one else. It is magical I can feel the years of your life etched here on the rocks of the river. He gave you this gift, and you have taken us on the first step of our journey towards the treasure.'

The three of them stood looking across the fast-flowing water. The river had not yet frozen, but icicles reached down from the bank. Magnus was concentrating very hard on the riverbed. 'Alva,' he said, 'did you and Bjorn ever carve any runes yourselves?'

'No, we would look at the images that were here already, but didn't add any ourselves.'

'Well, look here,' he replied, directing her a few paces up stream. 'It took me a while to see it, but there is a fresh carving.' Magnus gestured at a scratched symbol on the nearest rock. Alva looked at the runes.

'I can make out your name, Uncle. But look next to them. There is a further symbol. ᛈ My "joy". . . This must be directing us to the next location —somewhere that is your "joy"?'

Her uncle threw his arms in the air. 'I've got it! From when we were very little there was a ridge that looked out between Giant's Finger and Dwarf's Finger. Between the two mountains is a view of the water, the trees, the crags of the cliffs . . . It always made me think of a cup of plenty. The valley between the mountains was like a goblet into which the gods had poured all beauty and goodness. We went there many times together. It was the place I always felt the most joy. These certainly are directions.'

'And the runes continue,' Brianna said. 'Look, here's another one, and another.' True enough, on stones set along the bank, the runes were repeated. They were small—only about the size of the palm of Alva's hand—but now her mother had pointed them out they were clear.

'Your father!' Brianna said, with a glint in her eyes and a smile curling around her lips. 'He has such a mischievous spirit. Only he would have thought to cover Giant's Finger with our names! Such a romantic.'

'They're leading us on,' Alva said excitedly. She ran her fingers over the runes, and as she did so, she could almost see her father, crouched over and concentrating, carving their names with his family fixed in his mind. The thought warmed her through. 'Let's go to your place of joy, uncle,' she said, raising her torch higher and sweeping it ahead of them.

I

A Creeping Cold

They turned right, away from the river, and began climbing again. In front, Alva could see the smaller mountain, Dwarf's Finger, looming out of the night. It was covered in snow and looked unwelcoming. Alva had never trusted the little mountain, preferring to stay on the slopes of Giant's Finger, which she knew so well.

At a point between the two mountains, the river ran into an estuary, which made a pool of water that reflected the peaks above like a mirror.

'I was always fascinated by the ridge over there which connects the two mountains. It's called Giant's Sword,' Magnus explained.

'What is the legend of that place?' Alva asked. 'I know of it, but never heard the tale of how it got its name.'

'The story says that, when the giants were defeated at Kilsgard, one of them collapsed on his back, with his finger pointing up to the gods above in retribution. This became the mountain. But his sword fell by his side. The greedy dwarves tried to take it for themselves, but were also struck down by the men of the town—so they too point heavenward, with the sword lying between them.'

'It's treacherous to cross in winter,' Brianna said. 'I have made this journey many times with Bjorn, but when it's iced over, the ridge of Giant's Sword can be terrifying. There is a sheer drop on either side.'

'Well, my location is just on the other side. We must go carefully. Send Fenrir ahead and we will follow where he treads,' Magnus said.

Having left behind the river bank they climbed back up the sides of the mountain at a steep incline, keeping the water to their left as they moved forwards and upwards. There was no clear path to the causeway, but Magnus smashed through the low bracken and carved a way through. Ducking under a final tree, Alva saw the icy crossing ahead. It was only a stride wide, and her mother was right—it looked terrifying. Alva crouched down and spoke quietly to Fenrir.

'Fen, you've got to get us across here. Find the safest path and lead us.' She shuffled him forward, pointing over the white bridge. Understanding her meaning, he started to move slowly and cautiously forward. The three of them followed, Hraf constantly swooping overhead.

Alva could feel that the smooth soles on her worn, old shoes were useless on this surface. They kept slipping sideways, dragging her close to the edge. Below, the water was freezing. She would die if she fell. Alva knew she would have much better control using her bare feet. She could climb trees, scale mountains, walk across dangerous rocks—as long as she could feel the surface on her skin. Despite the risk of the cold encasing her and biting away at her insides, she crouched down, untied her shoes, removed her socks, and placed her bare soles onto the ice.

Her mother, already some way across the causeway, turned and saw what she was doing. 'Alva,' she cried out, 'do you want to lose your limbs? What are you doing?'

But Alva stood up, feeling more confident

that she could cross as she wrapped her toes around the uneven surfaces. It felt like an age, as they edged across the sheet of ice. Fenrir was attentive, moving back and forth to check that all three of them were still together. Twice she saw her mother slide forward, and on one occasion Magnus leapt backwards, grabbing her cloak as she moved dangerously close to the edge. But, eventually, they all made it across.

Once back on solid ground, Alva flung her arms around her mother and ruffled Fenrir's fur. 'Clever, brave wolf,' she whispered in his ear. She put her shoes carefully back onto her frozen feet. They were numb.

Hraf gave a noisy caw in celebration, then swooped down to settle on Magnus's shoulder. 'Shush, bird!' he scolded it. 'We don't want to be heard.' Yet he stroked the black feathers on Hraf's neck affectionately and the bird nestled his beak into Magnus's long hair for a moment, before taking off again.

'Did Father really bring you all this way, Mother?' Alva asked.

'He said it was a rite of passage,' Brianna replied. 'As we moved across the causeway, he said we were leaving behind our real selves and entering a place where we were eternal. Where our memories would be secret and safe for all time.'

'I guess that's romantic, really,' Magnus said, with a huff. 'My brother always knew the right words to make a woman happy.'

Alva thought it was lovely.

Turning to Magnus, Brianna asked, 'So where is your site, this place of your joy?'

'It's just up this ridge a little,' Magnus said, guiding them higher up Dwarf's Finger. As they walked, the first light of dawn began to draw a line of colour across the horizon.

'It's nearly time for the Jarl's men to rouse the town,' Brianna said. 'We must move fast. They will lumber behind us for a while, but with every moment we are losing our advantage.'

They picked up their pace.

Finally they reached a level point on the mountainside. It was ringed with pine trees that stood like soldiers along the edge of the ridge. Behind these was a large tree trunk, lying on its side and ravaged by the passage of time. Magnus slowly moved towards it.

'I used to sit here as a young boy,' he said.

'From this spot you can see all of Giant's Finger, the river, the valley, and the lights of Kilsgard just in the distance. Many, many hours were spent gazing at this view.'

Brianna and Alva gave him a moment to soak up the atmosphere. Fenrir sniffed around the site, but seemed to find nothing to interest him. Alva spoke up, 'Uncle, if this was the place Father was thinking of then surely, like he did at my site, he would have carved mother's name here and set a trail to her site?'

Magnus roused himself, his eyes alight at the prospect of searching for clues. 'You're right Alva,' he said. 'Let's turn our torches to the ground and find Bjorn's messages.'

They began sweeping their flames from side to side, although the increasing brightness of the impending morning was growing, and glowing along the outlines of the trees. They searched.

'Has anyone found anything?' Magnus asked after some time.

'Nothing,' they replied. Alva was panicking slightly. Had they misread her father's clue? Were they on the wrong trail?

Then Fenrir started to scratch excitedly at a rock near to the tree trunk. Alva went to him and

examined it, aware that his sensitive nose must have found some faint trace of her father. Carved into the stone were the two runes signifying her mother's name, and a third one: ⌠

Brianna walked over and stared with wide eyes at the carving.

'I already thought I knew the special place Bjorn has in mind for me, so I am not surprised to find this symbol. The rune eihwaz ⌠: the yew tree.

'When Bjorn first brought me to Kilsgard, I was mourning for my life and my family in Ireland. He said that the yew was the tree of death and of new life. He took me to a huge yew that hangs from the edge of Dwarf's Finger. He carved my runes into its bark, and told me we should return to that place with every new chapter in our life. We did, when we were bound together as man and wife, when you were born, Alva, and when Ivan arrived. With every momentous occasion we returned to the yew tree, and again Bjorn would carve my runes into its bark. Its trunk is covered with my name. That is the place he means.'

'Well, if it's precious to you, Mother,' Alva replied, 'then that's why Father is sending us there. Do you remember the way?'

'I do,' she replied. Tugging her red hair back from her face, she pulled her cloak around her tightly, and said to the others. 'Come with me.'

Taking one last look back past Giant's Finger, Alva saw something that stopped her in her tracks. 'Look!' she cried. 'Isn't that Kilsgard down there?' She could see the outlines of the wooden gates and the fences which surrounded the town, but what alarmed her was the lights pricking on, appearing as they watched. She could see the large hall, its shape carved into the darkness by a wreath of fiery torches. Smaller flames were moving, and houses were springing to life. 'They are awake,' she said. 'They will be scouring the mountain soon.'

The three fell silent as Brianna ran forward into the trees ahead. 'This way,' she almost screamed back to them.

The woods were much denser here, but the group was driven on by fear and determination. They were climbing higher and higher, making for the peak of Dwarf's Finger. 'Mother, how much further is it?' Alva called ahead.

'We are getting closer,' came the reply.

Inside her shoes, Alva's feet were still feeling

heavy with cold and pain. Occasionally she felt the slash of a thorny nettle or the whip of a branch, and it reassured her that she still had sensation in her legs. Once that left her, the bite of the ice would take over, creeping through her toes, up her legs, until they would become useless. She didn't want to think of that. It was a cruel and painful way to lose limbs.

The incline became steeper, until the three of them had to use their hands to crawl up the sheer rock. They slipped and slid their way over the granite hulks, as Fenrir stood above, pulling at a garment, or pacing anxiously. Alva could feel exhaustion sweeping down her body. She had not slept enough, she had not eaten enough, and she was frozen through to her bones. She really did not want to carry on. But as she stopped, clinging to the cliff face, she felt Fenrir pull at her collar. He turned his watery eyes on her, and Alva felt the warmth of his love rush through her like a wave.

Pulling herself up, she continued her ascent.

'We're here!' called Brianna from somewhere above. Alva hauled herself over a final rock and there she saw the peak of Dwarf's Finger. Ahead was the sea, wrapping itself around the base of the mountain like a cloak. The coast continued its peaks and valleys to the north, while Alva looked and saw the top of Giant's Finger looming still larger behind them. 'This is the place,' Brianna said quietly.

At the very highest point of the mountain stood a battered, huge, and solid yew tree. Alva thought its trunk must be three times the width of her outstretched arms. Brianna walked over to the ancient tree and put her hands on its ice-covered bark. She was very still. Alva walked up to her mother and could see she had streaks of tears rolling down her cheeks. 'Mother,' she said, 'why are you crying?'

'Oh, daughter,' replied Brianna, grabbing Alva and pulling her into a tight embrace. The warmth of her mother rushed through Alva, even warming her frozen feet. 'Your father has brought us here and I don't know why. But he's not here himself. I miss him so much. I can't imagine that I will never see him again.'

Alva was crying too now. 'I don't think he's gone,' she sobbed into her mother's cloak. 'These messages make it feel as if he is speaking to us right now. He's guiding us and talking to us from across the seas. We must make him

proud, and we must follow his guidance.'

Brianna had one hand stretched out against the tree. 'Look,' she said, 'here's my name.' Alva focused on the bark and was stunned. She saw the now familiar shapes of the Ophila rune and the apple, but they were not carved once. They were carved a thousand times. Again and again, on every piece of the tree, those symbols appeared in the dawn light.

'He loves you so much,' Alva whispered.

Brianna caught her breath, turned and wiped her cheeks. 'And I love him,' she said, a new strength in her voice. 'As at the lake, I imagine Bjorn has left another clue. Cast your eyes about and let's begin the final unknown journey. From here, we do not know what lies ahead.'

Alva set to searching; scouring the ground and poring over every rock and branch. Then she saw it—a single sign that would have been easily missed. A single rune: ᚷ. It was scratched into a rock near the tree.

'Gebo?' Brianna said. 'It means "gift". But this surely doesn't guide us to a particular location. Where does he want us to go? Magnus, do you know? I've never been further than this tree.'

Magnus scratched his beard. 'That side of the mountain is barren and wind-swept, since it looks out over the sea. I can think of little there.'

Alva felt a thought drop like a stone into her mind. A memory began to play out, as if it was taking place right there in front of her on the ridge. She let out a loud, long laugh, but her laughter was cut short as another sound rode to them on the wind. They could hear the distant shouts of men.

After a long pause she spoke.

'I know why father left this rune here. I've just remembered something from when I was younger; perhaps only seven or eight winters? I think it is the final location. One night, Father and I went out late, wandering in the mountains. Winter was approaching, but we were still full of the adventures of the autumn months, so Father said we could explore further than usual, and leave Giant's Sword for this side of the mountain.

'We crossed the peak, but a fast snowstorm came in from the west. It covered the mountain, and made it impossible to return home. Father was anxious but tried to make it fun for me. He said we were like the Viking explorers of old, venturing into unknown northern lands and finding sanctuary in the snow. We searched for shelter in the caves that look out over the waters. There is a network of them along the cliff face. We huddled for warmth, and Father made a fire. All night he told me stories and reassured me that we would be able to get home safely once the storm passed. It was terrifying, but good to be together.

'When we got home the next morning, Father said that I should not worry you with our adventure, and it would be our secret. He told you that he had drunk too much mead and the two of us had fallen asleep at Ingeld's house. But when we spoke of our adventure, he said that the cave had been a gift to us from the gods, in our time of need, and he would always treasure our time there together. I am sure this is where he is leading us, and that this is where he has hidden the treasure.'

Alva felt her heart racing with excitement.

'And do you remember the runes?' she continued, 'There was an instruction about a "dark place beneath a birch". I remember there was a tree by the entrance to the cave we slept in. But was it a birch?'

Magnus raised his voice now. 'There are many

caves down there, Alva,' he said. 'We will have to move carefully. Can you pore through your mind-hoard and remember the exact location? We must move fast, since the men of Kilsgard are getting closer.'

'I'll try,' Alva said, as her mother took her by the hand. Brianna looked reproachfully at Alva. This was yet another time she had been deceived by her daughter and husband. But there was no time for retribution, as every moment the sounds of the men on the mountain were drawing closer. They continued down the side of the mountain.

The ground was much rockier now, with fewer trees. The sea smashed against the base of Dwarf's Finger as a constant reminder not to lose balance. Even Fenrir was feeling unsure as he moved sideways down the steeper parts of the rock face. Hraf had vanished, but Magnus was too preoccupied with getting to the caves to show much concern.

With each strong gust of wind they could hear the very faint sound of the men scouring Giant's Finger. Yet, even as they were concentrating particularly hard on not losing their footing, they heard a new sound. Different voices. A man and a woman. And they were very near. Perhaps only the other side of the rocks.

They all stood frozen to the spot. Looking back towards her uncle, Alva mouthed, 'We've found the criminals!'

My Home is my Castle

'I'm sure I can hear it!' The woman's voice was high and agitated. 'It sounds like a lot of men. They are looking for you. I knew this would happen! It was only a matter of time before they went out in search of you. We need to get out of here. Let's just leave the treasure and head for the boat. At least we will escape with our lives.'

'Hush, woman,' spoke a deep, strong voice. 'We have not come this far to leave frustrated. It has to be one of these caves and we've searched most of them now. If there are men on Giant's Finger, it will take them time to reach us here. I am not giving up. We leave with the treasure, or we die trying.'

Alva looked at Magnus. He had fury in his eyes, and his fists were balled up. Like her, he recognized their voices.

The woman spoke again, this time even nearer to where they were hiding. 'You are a gold-hungry fool, Ingeld. I wish I had never agreed to help you with this. It is pure madness. And the men haven't eaten for some time. They could perish in this cold tonight.'

The voice was Gudrun's; her mother's closest friend. Alva had been worried about her at the sacrifice, as she seemed so fragile, but she shouldn't have been concerned. Gudrun was part of this mystery. And so was her husband, Ingeld—their father's travelling companion, friend to Magnus and Bjorn from childhood, trusted by their family. When had he returned to their lands? It was he who had taken the men. It was he who had set out to find the treasure. It was he who half the village was now seeking. Betrayal cut like a knife.

'I don't care about the Englishmen,' Ingeld answered aggressively. 'They have been next to useless. The monk could translate some of the runes I could not, but he could not get me any closer to the final location. They were a waste of time and by taking them I drew attention to my own search for Bjorn's treasure. Let them rot.'

Suddenly, unexpectedly, Magnus reared up over the rock. He nearly howled the word, 'Ingeld!'

Without thinking, Alva ran after her uncle, and her mother followed, shouting, 'Alva, no!'

There they were, face to face with the criminals who had put Kilsgard through so much fear. Ingeld looked terrible. He was stick thin, his beard was huge and dishevelled, and he was dirty from top to toe. He had the look of a wild man about him. Beside him was Gudrun. Brianna locked eyes with her.

'Gudrun!' she said. 'But I only just saw you at the sacrifice. What are you doing up here? What is going on? Is Bjorn with you, Ingeld?'

Gudrun didn't get a chance to reply, as Ingeld let out a huge holler. 'Ha ha ha! My dear, dear friends!' he said moving towards them. 'How I have longed to see you!'

'Stop,' Magnus replied. 'Come no further.'

'What?' said Ingeld. 'No welcome for an old friend? It has been many months since we last saw each other and I thought you might be pleased to see me.'

'Pleased?!' Alva rushed to the front. 'Where is my father? You left together, yet here you are sneaking around the mountains alone. Where is he?' She was shouting now, as anger flooded through her veins. 'Tell me where he is!'

'I will not be spoken to like this, Alva,' Ingeld said, edging closer. 'You have known me since you were a babe in arms. You should show me a little more respect.'

'Respect?' It was Brianna speaking now, outrage coursing through her voice. 'Like the respect you showed to the two Englishmen you carried away in the night? Like the respect you showed my husband by trying to take treasure he has concealed? You want us to respect you now, Ingeld?'

'I can explain.' Gudrun was speaking now, through desperate tears. 'I didn't mean to betray your family's trust.'

Alva gave a scornful laugh, her heart burning with vengeance.

Gudrun continued, 'I knew nothing of Ingeld's return until two nights ago when he came to the house, in darkness. I felt the Norns cut the strands of my life there and then as I saw him, I was so afraid. At first I thought he was a ghost, but my fear increased when he told me of his plans. He said he needed me to keep my ears open in Kilsgard, as he was planning to secure us great riches. Ingeld said we would leave here and find a new place to live, where we could enjoy the spoils. He is my husband. I had to help him. But I have been horrified by what he has done. Please forgive me.'

Gudrun fell at Brianna's feet, reaching towards her, with tears coursing down her cheeks. She looked pitiful.

'Forgiveness is not for tonight, Gudrun,' Brianna replied in a steely voice. 'Tonight is about answers. Answers and vengeance.'

'Ha!' Ingeld laughed heartily. Always the weaker man next to her father, Alva thought Ingeld now looked wretched and small. His beard was knotted and foul, too, but the large arm muscles beneath his linen shirt reminded her that he was still strong. A Viking. 'You think you have cause for vengeance? And why might that be, Brianna?'

It was her mother's turn to laugh now. 'Well, firstly you have not returned with Bjorn. You must have betrayed him and abandoned him. For this you will pay.' She took a step towards Ingeld. 'And secondly, you are up here, searching for a treasure you know belongs to him and his family. You have no right to it, yet you seek it for yourself. If that is not cause for vengeance, I don't know what is!'

Ingeld moved a step towards her. They were now just a few paces from each other. 'Oh, you see this tale in such a narrow way. Here I am, betrayer of your beloved Bjorn, ready to snatch wealth away from the hands of his dear family. We went to Lindisfarne together, and were bringing back wealth for all the people of Kilsgard. I saw when he and Magnus took the monk's treasure from under the stone floor of their church. It was not his to keep, but at the time I thought they were mad—who would want treasure that doesn't sparkle?

'Once Bjorn and I found ourselves on our travels to Constantinople, I realized the Christians were obsessed with their dead saints. Everywhere, they were honouring bits of bone, and I started to realize why Bjorn had taken these treasures to Kilsgard. He wanted to sell them and make himself and his family very rich. I asked him about the bones, and he said he had hidden them. This felt like a betrayal—to me, and to all of Kilsgard.'

'None of this excuses you, Ingeld,' Magnus

said. 'It just makes you more guilty. If you thought the treasures were not rightfully Bjorn's, you could have told Jarl Erik about them. But perhaps the real reason for your guilt is that you abandoned Bjorn. Where is he, and how did you end up back here without him?'

'I don't know where Bjorn is,' Ingeld replied. 'And if you think I betrayed him, you can judge for yourselves. I will tell you why I am back here alone. When I asked him about the treasure from Lindisfarne, he drew out that damned casket and showed me how he had created a riddle to conceal its whereabouts. He was so pleased with himself. He even told me that the casket was supposed to bring you three closer together. We all could see that poverty and conflict were driving a wedge between your perfect little family, and Bjorn was so excited about returning to Kilsgard and setting you on this challenge.'

Magnus was striding slowly up and down, while Alva's jaw was beginning to ache from clenching her teeth so tightly. Brianna alone stood still like a statue, staring at Ingeld.

He continued his speech. 'At night, Bjorn was constantly whittling away at the blasted casket, carving little serpents and adding details. He wanted it perfect for when he got back from this journey. It was to be his ultimate gift to you all. I wanted to decode the runes myself. But no matter how long I looked at the thing, I could not understand all of them. I was so angry and frustrated, and these feelings festered as we continued our journey together.'

Ingeld was in full flow now, pacing around in front of them as he continued his speech.

'One night, in a tavern in Francia, I saw a monk and an English earl tucked away, drinking in a corner. I was full of beer, and had lost sight of Bjorn earlier that day, so I sidled up to the strangers' table and struck up a conversation. They were reluctant to talk to me, recognizing me as a Viking. They were silent, so I drank more, happy to be in the company of outsiders like myself. The more I consumed, the looser my tongue became. I do not remember all of what I said, but in my boasts I think I mentioned the objects taken from Lindisfarne and Bjorn's infuriating casket.

'The men said nothing while I spoke. The earl asked but one question: "And will you both be sleeping here in the tavern tonight?"

"Drunk and senseless, I replied that we

had lodgings above. When I awoke the next morning, I found the door to our room open. Our belongings had been ransacked, and when I saw that Bjorn's bags were now empty, a rush of fear flew through me. My loose tongue had lost him the casket. It was nowhere to be seen. Bjorn's bed was empty, and I realized I had not set eyes on him all night.'

'Why?' Alva interrupted. 'Where was he? Where had he gone?'

'That I don't know, little lady,' Ingeld drawled. 'He had been acting strangely the whole time we were in Francia but these were yet more secrets he hid from me, his friend.

'When I found the casket was stolen, in a thrill of vengeance I stormed out through the town, asking everyone I met if they had seen the English monk and his companion. No one had any word of them, apart from a stinking old man at the abbey, who said that, yes, a monk of the English monastery of Lindisfarne had stayed there with an armed man, but that they had left by horse in the night.

'I knew exactly where they were heading. They were following the runes. I immediately began a long and hard journey back north. I had heard no word from Bjorn, and while I was sorry to abandon my friend, I knew he would be after my blood if he heard what I'd told these English strangers.

'As I travelled alone, I came across all sorts of trials. No one likes a lone Viking, and it was a perilous trek back to Kilsgard. But all along the route I asked after the monk and earl. They were a few steps ahead of me at every turn. When I reached Kilsgard, I stayed in the mountains. I did not want to reveal myself to you or to the people of Kilsgard. I knew you would ask me a perilous set of questions. I had left Bjorn and the other men. I had no news of where Bjorn had gone. In fact, I had a feeling something bad had happened to him that night in Francia.

'Instead, I stayed on Giant's Finger, alone, searching for his treasure so that Gudrun and I could escape the village and start again somewhere new. But I needed the casket to get the full set of clues. I watched the Englishmen as they camped, and when they were asleep I took the earl and casket with me. But it was broken— missing its lid—so I went back for the monk, as I was sure he had the final piece. He didn't, and the two of them were of no use at all. I should have killed them, but by then I had asked for the help of my wife, and Gudrun pleaded for their lives.'

Gudrun was still lying on the ground crying, while Brianna continued to stare coldly at Ingeld. Alva was amazed that they were all simply listening to this terrible criminal, rather than attacking him. But still she remained rooted to the spot, desperate to know more.

'The Englishmen are tied up in one of the caves, and can become food for the wolves, for all I care,' he said. 'So that is how I came to be here, and that is why I have earned this treasure. You knew nothing of it. I have gone through trials and tribulations to gain it for myself. Now step aside, and let me continue my search.'

Instead of stepping aside, Alva took another step forward. 'Where is my father?' she asked again.

'I don't know what happened to Bjorn in Francia. I know he had planned to meet with someone in secret that day. I was upset by his betrayal, which was what drove me to drink so much that night. But he never returned to the tavern, and I have heard no word of him since. As time has passed, I have realized Bjorn was never my true friend. He was keeping secrets from me at every turn. Good riddance to him, I say.'

These sneering words cut into Alva like a knife and she felt anger sear through her insides. 'How dare you,' she said, striding straight for Ingeld.

As if by reflex, the Viking drew his sword and wielded it at her. But Alva had such a fire burning inside her that she lunged at him, regardless of the blade. 'I don't want to hurt you, girl,' Ingeld said, turning on his toes and raising the sword up high between them.

But Alva felt her anger spill over, and again she began to rush at Ingeld.

As she came close to the tip of his sword, Fenrir suddenly pounced from behind the rocks.

He hit Ingeld hard on his side, toppling him into the snow. The sword fell from his hands, and tumbled away to rest at Brianna's feet.

Together, Alva and Magnus landed on top of Ingeld, and despite his struggles, turned him onto his front.

Gudrun had been screaming throughout all this, and now ran to her husband. 'Please, don't hurt him,' she said. 'He has done wrong, but he didn't kill those men. He just got greedy. If you give him to the Jarl, he will be sentenced and punished. If you let us leave, we will cause no more harm for anyone in Kilsgard. We have a small boat, just down there. We can be gone in minutes and you will hear no more from us. Please, Brianna, our families have been so close for so many years. I helped you bring Alva and Ivan into the world. If you would only give us this last chance?'

'No!' Alva cried. 'You heard what he said about my father. And he left him. Ingeld abandoned him and followed his own greed. He has to be punished.'

But Alva felt her uncle relax his grip on Ingeld. 'The problem is, Alva, we cannot drag him back across Giant's Sword. We still have to rescue the

Englishmen, and we have our own investigations to complete. To keep Ingeld hostage will hold us up. And although I agree he has betrayed us and deceived the town, we have been friends for many years. I don't want to see him tried by the townsfolk. They are baying for blood and he would not survive. Something also tells me that Ingeld's life is of more value to us than his death.'

Horrified, Alva looked over at her mother.

Brianna was still staring at her friend intently. Then she simply nodded her head and turned away. 'Go,' she said quietly, but she picked up the sword by her feet as she did so. 'I have your sword, Ingeld, and I will use it against either of you if you try to attack us. I do not fear drawing your blood. Go from here, and never return. If you can do something useful with your lives, do so. Now run!' She spun the sword over her head, its blade catching the light of sunrise as it swooped over her.

Magnus pulled Alva back from Ingeld, and the beaten man raised himself to his feet. Gudrun took him firmly by the hand and pulled him away.

'You have shown mercy,' Ingeld said. 'I would

not have shown you that kindness. Thank you.'
Then they turned and scrambled away, down
the side of the cliff towards the water.

Alva rounded on her mother. 'What have you
done? Without him, we cannot show the Jarl
who was responsible for taking the Englishmen.
We will be suspects. And did you not want to
punish him for betraying Father?'

'Be calm, Alva,' her mother said. 'Old
friendships are never pure. They move through
turbulent waves, and you carry one another like
ships through dangerous waters. Gudrun and
Ingeld have carried our family many times. This
one last time we can carry them. We can let them
try their fortunes on the oceans, alone.'

Then Magnus spoke, 'You are right about the
Jarl, but we will have the monk and earl. We will
have to rely on them as witnesses, and the fact
that Gudrun has left Kilsgard so suddenly in
the night will aid our case. If we tried to retain
Ingeld, we would have had to stop our search for
Bjorn's treasure, when we are so close. Now we
have a small pocket of time left to see if we can
succeed. I can hear the Jarl's men getting closer;
we don't have long. But I think the first thing we
have to do is find the missing men. We cannot

leave them starving and cold on the mountain, and now they must act as witnesses for us.'

Still thirsty for revenge, glowering inside at her mother and uncle's weakness, but nevertheless spurred into action, Alva began clambering amongst the craggy rocks on the side of the mountain. The mouths of hundreds of caves gaped towards the sea, and were connected by networks of tunnels that ran through the heart of the mountain. Alva thought she would return here with Fen when this drama was over, and explore them more thoroughly. But for now, she was on a hunt. She called out for the Englishmen, and, after peering into the mouths of ten or so caves, she heard a faint reply.

'Here!' Alva cried. Scrambling further along she saw a particularly large entrance, with a fire still burning inside. She crept closer, then called out, 'Uncle, Mother! I've found them.'

Two bodies were hunched up against the far wall: Wiglaf of Bamburgh and Edmund of Lindisfarne. They looked cold, terrified, and hungry, but they were alive. Both had clots of blood on their temples, where Ingeld had struck them and knocked them out. Their hands were tied behind their backs.

'Are you friends?' Wiglaf asked tentatively.

Alva recognized the English word 'friend', and replied, 'Yes. Friends. More are on their way, but there are just three of us up here right now. The man and woman who imprisoned you have fled. You are safe.'

Seeming to grasp the sense of her Old Norse babble, Wiglaf gave a deep sigh of relief, but the monk Edmund seemed even more agitated.

Magnus and Brianna rounded the edge of the cave mouth, with Fenrir in tow. The two men crawled further into the darkness of the cave when they saw the wolf, but Alva tried to reassure them. 'He's my wolf,' she said. 'He is a friend.'

Magnus stepped towards the men slowly, showing his empty hands as a sign he was no threat. In English he said to them, 'It is good to see you both.' Wiglaf seemed surprised that he spoke to them in their own tongue. 'We have been looking for you,' Magnus continued. 'You are in no danger now. The man who took you is gone, and more help is on its way.'

Edmund the monk was still upset though. With Magnus translating his words to Alva and Brianna, he said, 'If that foul man who

imprisoned us has gone, he has taken any chance we had of finding my monastery's treasures. They are worth a thousand times what my poor life is worth. It was all I could pray for that we might find them and return them to their home.'

'You haven't lost every chance of finding them,' Alva replied, smiling now. 'Come with us, help us, and you might yet find them tonight.' She went to the bound men and cut their ropes with her knife. Freed at last, the two stretched their arms and legs, wringing feeling back into their hands. They stood up slowly and came forward.

'I am Wiglaf, Earl of Bamburgh and thegn of King Edwin of Northumbria,' the first said.

Speaking to Magnus, the second said, 'We met before. I am Edmund, brother of the monastery of Lindisfarne.'

The two Englishmen looked very close in age, and each had probably seen about twenty or so winters. Alva wondered if they were related, as they had similar angular, handsome features. However, one was dressed in the finery of an English knight, while the other wore a simple, brown hooded gown, covering him from head to foot.

'Although you are our enemies in so many ways,' Wiglaf said, 'we are pleased to see you. We could not have survived another night in this cave with no food. We are grateful to you.'

Magnus replied, 'We are pleased to see you too, as we had feared you were dead. We know why you are here in Kilsgard, and we know you were following the clues carved on a casket. But I want to know how you came to learn of this object.'

Edmund cleared his throat, 'we were not intending to travel north. When your men came to my island you left it ragged and poor. We had no money left to rebuild our monastery and had lost our most precious relics. The abbot wanted me to travel on the continent and try to secure the bones of another saint, who could become the focus for a new church we would build on the island. My brother is an earl of the Northumbrian court,' he said, gesturing at Wiglaf. So they were brothers. 'He agreed to accompany me, and we set off south, with all the maps and resources our monastery could spare.

'We stayed at Christian sites across England, and after crossing the waters to Francia, found that we were well looked after wherever we travelled. But when we were staying in Rheims, our journey took a different turn. A drunk Viking, that man who imprisoned us, came over. He would not leave, and his speeches turned my stomach. In his ghastly Viking slurs, he told us of his time in our isles, where he slaughtered my brothers and stole our treasures. We could not understand all of what he spoke, but we recognized that he knew where our relics were, and he had a casket of clues which could lead us to them.

'This was fuel to the fire for myself and my brother. We wanted to retrieve Lindisfarne's treasures with every fibre of our beings. So, while the man was lying drunk on his bed, we found the casket and escaped.'

We had to change our plans of travelling to Constantinople, and instead we rode north. The trouble began when we got here, to this godforsaken land. It is so hostile. It's like the mountain wants to defeat and destroy us. We thought we were lost. But now you are here and perhaps we have a second chance.'

Magnus had listened carefully, relaying the story to Brianna and Alva in their own tongue. Eventually he turned to the Englishmen and said, 'We may have the final clues to find the treasure. The runes on the casket were encrypted so that only we three would be able to read them. The man who made the casket was my brother, Brianna's husband, and Alva's father, Bjorn. He chose locations only we would know, and we are now very close to the final place. Will you come with us?'

Edmund's eyes lit up in delight. 'We might get to see the relics? Of course we will come with you. We are your humble servants. If I can cast my eyes on those precious objects one more time, I will die with a happy heart.'

'Well, let's hope none of us dies today,' Magnus answered.

To Give from Afar

The sound of men's shouts was getting ever closer. The sun was now turning the sky pink and red in a blaze of colour over the snow-white mountains. From the side of the mountain they could just make out a tiny boat with two figures inside it, rowing frantically away towards the sea.

'Ingeld and Gudrun are free,' Brianna said, looking out. 'I wish them well.'

Alva glowered at her mother's words. Her heart was still set on revenge. But right now, her mind was focused on finding the treasure her father had so carefully concealed. Brianna looked down at Alva gently. 'Daughter, where is this cave you and your father hid in?'

Alva ruffled her red hair thoughtfully. 'I was very young. I'm not entirely sure, but I know it had a ring of stones near the entrance.'

The monk spoke up. 'If you remember from the inscriptions there was mention of a birch tree. We should perhaps find a cave with a birch nearby.'

'But there are so many,' Brianna grumbled. 'How will we find it before the men make it across to us? This is our riddle to solve. We need to finish this. If they get here before we find Bjorn's treasure we will have to stand back while the Karls take control'

Magnus spoke again. 'Bjorn had left trails from our different locations. We have not been very good at following them, but if we retrace our steps to where we last saw your name engraved, Brianna, perhaps we might find a path to the cave.'

All agreed this was as good a plan as any, so they retraced their steps back to where they had grappled with Ingeld, and over the top of the rocks. There they found Bjorn's now familiar scratchings. 'Look forward a few steps, everyone,' Magnus instructed. 'Can you see any others?'

Wiglaf cried out, 'Here!' Another rock had the *gebô* rune carved on it. So they picked up the pace again, walking in a line with Fenrir at the head, each trying to avoid the sheer drops that loomed to their left. They were wrapping right around the back of Dwarf's Finger now, and here the rocks were even more sheer, with the open sea howling below.

'This feels familiar,' Alva said thoughtfully.

Suddenly a clearing appeared in the face of the mountain. There, as she had described, was a ring of stones around the edge of the open space. And, proudly reaching towards the skies, right by the entrance to a cave stood a huge, magnificent, ancient birch tree. No one spoke. They all knew this was it.

Alva was the first to move. She crunched over the snow, down the incline towards the cave ahead. It was smaller than the one they had found the Englishmen inside. This was more of a tunnel than a hollowed-out space. The others followed her. 'It looks small and dark,' she said.

'Look,' Edmund cried out. He was pointing at a carving to the right of the cave entrance. 'What does this say?'

Magnus peered down at the rock and took his magnifying glass out of his pouch. 'Help me examine this carving, Alva,' her uncle said,

calling her forward.

There was a line of runes here and they formed a full sentence. He read the phrase aloud. 'They say, "Well done, brother, wife, daughter. Here is my gift to you. Do with it what you will".'

They had reached the final location and they had found where Bjorn had been leading them.

'We must go inside, but it's too narrow for all of us,' Magnus said. 'I think me, Alva and Fenrir should go in, while you three stay out here on guard.'

Alva interjected, 'Uncle, whatever is inside this cave once belonged to Edmund and his brothers. I think he should come with us too.' Magnus looked suspiciously at the monk, but then nodded tersely. 'Okay, but let's hurry. The men must be on Dwarf's Finger by now.'

Fenrir went first, with Alva behind, then Magnus wielding a torch, and Edmund at the back. Brianna and Wiglaf stayed outside the cave. Alva's mother was still wielding the huge sword she had claimed from Ingeld.

The passage was narrow, but then widened out into a larger chamber. Alva paused for a moment, her childhood memory again replaying vividly in her mind. 'Now I remember,' she said.

'Father thought this was a good cave because any approaching wolves would have to come down the passage and we could simply place a fire at its mouth. He was so clever . . .'

She wiped a tear from her cheek as Magnus placed a reassuring hand on her shoulder. 'He's not here right now,' he said, 'but your mother and I are. We are a family, and by working together as a family we have got this far. Take strength in that.'

As her eyes adjusted to the darkness, Alva could just make out something hidden in a crag at the back. 'What's that?' she said, pointing.

Their eyes were struggling in the the dim light, but now they could all see something carved on a circular stone at the back of the chamber. Alva moved closer. It was simply one rune, carved large and coloured with red. It was the cross, X *gebô*; gift.

Alva murmured, 'I think we've found it.' She tried to shift the stone, but it weighed too much. Magnus joined her, heaving with all his strength. It moved a little, but would not shift sideways. Finally Edmund came to join them. Together they put their weight behind the stone and, with shouts of encouragement from Magnus, they moved it, bit by bit, to the side. Alva shone the torch inside.

Despite her uncle's description of the bones they had brought back from Lindisfarne, Alva had still hoped to see a pile of gold, rubies, sapphires, emeralds, cups, weapons, and coins. But what she saw was a wooden box, like a small coffin. While not hungry for wealth, her heart sank at the thought that this was the legacy her father had left her. If he was lost, never to return to Kilsgard, how could she, her mother, and Ivan survive with this?

But then she took heart. Perhaps the box had other riches inside it? Excitedly, she cried to her uncle, 'Quick, get it out. I want to see what's inside the box.'

Magnus grabbed the fragile box by one end and started to drag it into the chamber. In the torchlight, Alva caught her breath. There, emerging from the gloom, carved on the end of the box, was a picture of a mother holding a baby. With a pang of childish anxiety she thought how much she wanted her mother to hold her right now. But she pushed the feeling down, and helped her uncle shift the box further out from the cavity where Bjorn had concealed it.

More carvings emerged on all sides of the box, and they were so confusing. Alva could see men with beards, people with wings, and on its sides she could make out both Latin letters and runes. 'This is more of a mystery than Father's casket,' she murmured to her uncle.

Magnus replied, 'This is what we took from Lindisfarne, and I think that's where he got the idea of carving his own little box with runes on it, for us. This was what the monks had hidden beneath their church, and this is what Edmund and Wiglaf have been searching for.'

Looking behind her, Alva saw that Edmund was on the floor. Concerned, she rushed over to him, worried that he was hurt or sick.

'Leave him,' Magnus said. 'He is praying.' Alva had heard that Christians prayed, but she never thought it would look so sad and pitiful. The monk was crying into the sandy earth on the floor of the cave. He lay with his full body pressed downwards.

'Edmund,' she said kindly. 'Your treasure. We've found it.' The monk slowly looked upwards, then pulled himself to a seated position. 'Do you know what this is?' he said, Magnus translating as he spoke. 'This box contains the bones of our most holy saintly king, Oswald. He was a hero to us, and his bones were the most sacred treasure our monastery possessed.'

'Can I look inside?' Alva asked.

Edmund shuddered, but nodded. 'Inside, you will find more treasures,' he said, looking away. Alva worked at the nail that held the lid in place, finally dislodging it sideways. There she saw something she had not seen before in her twelve winters on earth: the remains of a human. There was a skull, and alongside it an assortment of other bones. The sight of them sent a chill down Alva's spine.

'When did he die?' Alva asked the monk.

'He left us over one hundred years ago,' Edmund replied.

Arranged around the saint's bones she could see all manner of objects. There was a little book, covered in leather, a golden cross, but there was also a larger book, which glittered gold in the torchlight. Edmund edged forward, averting his eyes from the bones of the saint, and drew it out.

'This,' he said, 'is our most precious book. It is a gospel book full of the words of our god. To us, this is the most magical, precious, sacred of objects.'

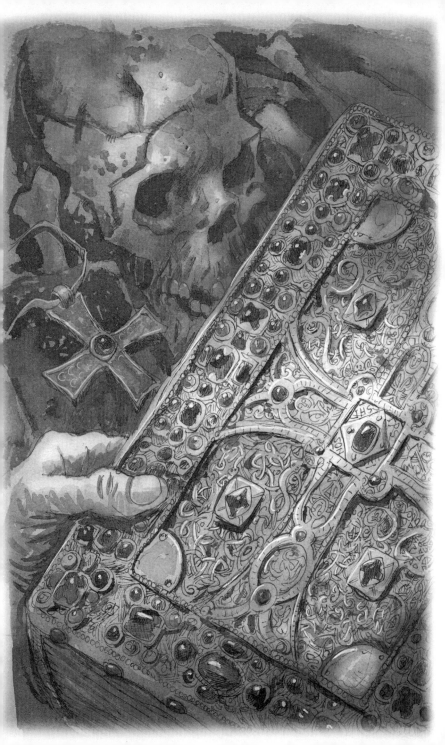

Alva looked at it. It was about five palms in height, and was bigger than the other books her uncle had showed her, but it had something even more magnificent about it. The entire outside was covered with gold and gemstones. Alva had the taste for gold and jewels that her fellow Vikings shared, and she could not take her eyes off the huge rubies, pearls, and gold leaf that covered the book. This was a treasure.

Magnus spoke, 'Edmund, you must help me take this outside to the clearing.' Together the men reversed down the narrow passageway, Fenrir and Alva leading the way. Eventually they emerged in the light. It was now bright, and the winter sun stood proudly above the horizon, warming the frozen mountainside.

Brianna and Wiglaf rushed over to see what treasures had emerged from the cave. The earl fell to his knees. The two brothers were now embracing, laughing and clapping each other on the back.

Once they had composed themselves, Edmund walked over to Magnus. In English he said, 'You are a wise man to have found this. Now I want to share something with you.' He had a rope tied around his middle, and he began to pick at some stitching around the side. Sown into the rope was a fragment of parchment. 'This was inside the casket when we took it that night in Rheims. I think it was meant for you.'

Magnus unfurled it and read. His face softened and he turned to his family. 'Alva, Brianna. This is from Bjorn. This is what he writes:

'"My dearest family. I love you so very much. Wherever I am in the world right now, I want you to know that you travel in my heart. I have adventures waiting for me, and I am not sure when I will return to you. But now you are the guardians of the treasure I took from England. The bones of the saint have rested heavy on me since I took them from Lindisfarne, and I am relieved I can now share this burden with you. I want the three of you to decide what happens to them. They could make you rich. But what I hope is that the journey to find them makes you even richer. I hope it shows you how together you are strong. All three of you need to work together. Magnus's logic, Brianna's loving heart, and Alva's wild spirit, combined, will solve the riddles I leave you. You must listen to each other, understand each other, and help each other when I am not with you. I love you and always will. B".'

It was the Vikings' turn to shed tears. Magnus thanked Edmund for sharing this with them, and relayed the contents of the note to him.

'So Father wanted us to decide,' Alva said. 'Well, I for one do not know what we could do with this. No doubt we could trade such valuable things to others and make a fortune.'

Magnus interjected, 'Relics are some of the most precious and expensive things Christians can buy. I have seen some trade all the wealth of their domain for a few fragments of bone. If we sold these we could be very rich.'

But Alva looked at the two men, who had now bowed their heads to the box and were quietly chanting Latin words. 'It means little to us,' she said, 'but it means so much to them. If someone were to come to Kilsgard and take away those items that hold us together—our statue of Odin, the Jarl's sword—I would hate them for it, and I would want them back. That is how these men feel. I would like to return the box to them.'

Brianna took three strides over to her daughter and flung her arms around her. 'Alva,' she said, 'you have a deep and compassionate soul. I was raised Christian, and I know what these bones mean to these men. I agree with you. I think they should be allowed to set sail safely from Kilsgard with their treasures.'

Magnus was reluctant. 'Bjorn and I took these together, as brothers, in the throws of a Viking raid. They are rightfully ours. We have very little wealth as a family, and this could help us become very rich. Also, the townsfolk would have us give them to Jarl Erik.' But looking at the women he bowed his head. 'I concede. Whatever you decide.'

Alva walked slowly over to the praying monk. His eyes were still wet with tears as she touched his shoulder, dragging him back to the moment. 'This is a gift,' she said, pointing at the box. 'For you.'

Edmund needed no translation. He sprung to his feet in pure joy. Magnus came over and explained to him in English what the three of them had decided. Edmund was clasping his hands together in sheer happiness, and Wiglaf simply beamed at them all. Then Edmund did something unexpected.

Opening the lid of the box once again, he pulled out the large book. He walked over to Alva and gestured towards her for her knife.

Alva passed the blade over, with complete trust in her heart. Edmund slowly, respectfully, and painstakingly began to prize the stones and gold plate from the front of the book. Slithers of gold and clumps of jewels fell in the snow around Alva's feet. She could see it hurt him to defile this book, but he removed every last fragment until it simply had boards and leather on the outside. Edmund looked up at Alva and said in Norse, 'our gift.'

Delighted, she scooped the precious objects up into her pouch, while the Englishmen began to lift the wooden box. At that point, she heard the familiar caw of Hraf in the sky above. He had been missing for a long while, but now he swooped down and settled gently on her shoulder. The black bird looked into her eyes and said in his half-human voice, 'Alva good.'

As they were preparing to depart, Alva heard the cries of her townsfolk.

'Who's there?' a voice called out.

Magnus replied, 'It is Magnus, Brianna, and Alva. We have found the missing men. They are safe. The criminal is banished. All is well. Approach without arms.'

The first face to appear was Kjartan, one of

the Jarl's most trusted karls. 'Magnus,' he said, 'you got here before us.'

'Yes,' Magnus replied. 'We followed the riddle of the runes, rather than the clamour of pride, and we have solved all that we set out to.'

'You have the two men, but where is the criminal?' Kjartan asked.

'There is much to tell you,' Magnus said. 'The criminal was none other than Ingeld.'

The group of men who were now gathered above the cave gave an audible gasp.

'Ingeld left Bjorn abroad and came back here to seek something my brother had concealed. We have found what that was. It is of no concern to you, good people. There is no gold, no wealth. Just the bones of a long-dead Christian. But it was precious to these Englishmen, and that is why they sought it. We must get this box, the men, and my tired family back to the Jarl so we can explain all. I hope there will be feasting tonight in celebration that we have put an end to the terrors which have assaulted Kilsgard.'

The men were still full of questions—some were hostile, demanding details of the treasure, and whether it belonged to the town, rather than to Bjorn's family—but Magnus silenced them.

'I will tell you the details as we return to the hall, but what you need to know now is that the manhunt is over. The town is safe.'

The armed men were all tired, and wanted to leave the snowy mountain, so for now they were content to be led by Magnus. They wanted to be out of the cold, back in their huts, and they followed his guidance. The box was surprisingly light, so Wiglaf and Edmund carried it easily between them, while the rest fell in single file as they made their way back to the warmth and safety of the town. The crossing over Giant's Sword was still treacherous, but the warmth of daylight made it feel a little safer.

As they returned to the familiarity of Giant's Finger, the Jarl's men called the rest of the men who were searching the mountain back to them, and as they approached the gates of Kilsgard they had formed quite a procession. Moving as one through the entrance, they wound towards the hall in the centre of the town. Jarl Erik was standing at its doors, haggard and worn-looking from the trials of the past two nights. He was surprised when he saw Magnus at the head of the crowd.

'You did not leave with the search party

Magnus,' he said.

'No, Erik,' Magnus replied. 'My family were following the runes, as I long explained to you within the hall. We knew where we had to go, and we knew it was where our anonymous criminal was heading too. I am particularly proud of my niece, Alva. Without her, we should never have solved this mystery.'

Alva beamed with pride as her mother squeezed her hand tightly.

Magnus continued. 'We found the missing men—look, they are alive and well. But we also found the source of all our town's woes these past few days. It was Ingeld.'

Erik was stunned. 'Ingeld is back from his travels? Where is he? Does he have news of our men who left here in spring? If he was responsible, he must be sorely punished!'

'Ingeld is gone,' Magnus replied. 'He escaped with Gudrun. You will understand when I explain the whole saga.'

Erik took Alva's uncle by the arm. 'Come inside Meginsalr and you must tell me everything.' Alva followed them, a feeling of exhausted elation coursing up and down her body. She had achieved so much in the past few days, and she felt changed by her experience. In fact, all her family were changed. Brianna was willing to let her have more freedom, and Magnus now fully appreciated her investigative skills. She had been through so much, and for a short time she had felt as if her father was still there, guiding her. Alva had completed this quest. Now it was time for another. Now her quest was to find out what had happened to Bjorn. She would find her father.

But as they all wound their way inside the hall, Alva finally felt warmth spread over her like a blanket. Magnus related all the details of their adventures, as servants poured out goblets of mead and passed around warming broth for everyone in the hall. He was beset with questions. Some men of the hall were distrustful of her uncle, some accused him of being involved in Ingeld's treachery, but Edmund helped greatly. He had learnt quite a few words of Norse, and, in broken phrases, he supported all that Magnus said. Slowly the atmosphere changed, becoming less charged, and more relaxed.

Alva felt really, deep-down tired. She went over to her mother and asked, 'Can I go home now? I need to sleep.'

The men continued to debate why Ingeld was allowed to leave, whether it was right to give the bones back to Edmund, what they were to do with the Englishmen now, and who the gold from the monk really belonged to. But Brianna took her daughter's hand and walked her back to their home, Fenrir trotting loyally behind them.

Inside, Alva lay down on the straw mattress, while her mother surrounded her with furs. There was still much to be determined, many questions to ask, and more action to take. But for now she wanted nothing but to sleep. Fenrir crawled onto the bed alongside her, and her mother took her by the hand. The last thing Alva heard, as she drifted into a world of dreams, was, 'I am so proud of you, my little shield maiden.'

Note on the runes used in the text:

Many of the runes in this story come from the Viking alphabet known as the 'Futhark'. An example of this can be found on the next page.

The Vikings did not use paper or parchment but would carve runes into stone, wood, or bone. They often used runes to mark their belongings, write messages, or to inscribe stone memorials commemorating loved ones.

The runes in this book are to be translated into modern English, and read from left to right. Original runic inscriptions from the period would have been written in Old Norse, and read from right to left.

Turn the page to study the Viking alphabet, maybe you could use it to write your own secret runic messages?

THE VIKING ALPHABET

f—fehu
Wealth
or
Cattle

u—ūruz
Strength of
will

þ—þurisaz
Thor
or
Giant

a—ansuz
Gods

h—hagalaz
Hail

n—naudiz
Need

i—īsaz
Ice

j—jēra
Year
or
Harvest

**t—tīwaz/
teiwaz**
Tyr

b—berkanan
Birch

e—ehwaz
Horse

m—mannaz
Man

'The runes are letters, but they are also words, and beyond that, they are stories.'—Alva

r–raidō
Ride
or
Journey

k(c)–
kaunan
Torch

g–gebô
Gift

W–wunjō
Joy

ï (æ)–
eihwaz
Yew tree

p–perþ
Pear tree

Z–algiz
Elk

S–sōwilō
Sun

l–laguz
Water
or
Lake

ŋ–ing-
waz
Freyr

d–dagaz
Day

O–ōþila
/ōþala
Heritage
or
Estate

VIKING GLOSSARY

CONSTANTINOPLE
Istanbul in Turkey was called Constantinople between 330 and 1453, and was once the capital of the Eastern Roman Empire.

FENRIR
A giant wolf, and son of the god Loki. Alva's pet wolf is named after him.

FRANCIA
A large kingdom in western Europe made up of parts of modern day France, Belgium, and Germany.

FREYA
The goddess of love. She wears a cloak made from falcon feathers, and rides into battle on a chariot pulled by cats.

FREYR
The god of peace, twin brother of Freya, and ruler of the elves.

IDUNNA

The goddess of spring, she is the keeper of the magic apples of immortality, which the gods must eat to preserve their youth.

JARL

A chief and wealthy nobleman who rules over a Viking territory.

JORMUNGAND

Known as the world serpent, he lies coiled around the world with his tail in his mouth, waiting for Ragnarok.

KARL

Not as rich or noble as a jarl, but not a slave either. Karls were free folk, and land owners.

LAGERTHA

A famous shield maiden of Norse sagas known for her bravery in battle.

LINDISFARNE

A small island off the coast of north-east England, home to Christian monks. It is known as the site of an infamous Viking raid in 793.

LOKI

The god of mischief and mayhem—a cunning trickster and shapeshifter.

NORNS

The three goddesses of destiny, who weave the strands of life, deciding the fate of all living beings.

NORTHUMBRIA

A medieval kingdom in what is now northern England and south-east Scotland.

ODIN

Ruler of all the gods, sometimes known as the All-father. He rides on an eight-legged horse called Sleipnir.

RAGNAROK

A string of chaotic events, including a great battle amongst the gods, that leads to the end of the world.

THOR

The hammer-wielding god of thunder, known for his great strength.

TYR

The warrior god of war and justice.

VALHALLA

Half of the Viking warriors who die in battle are chosen to spend their afterlife in Valhalla, an enormous hall, ruled over by the god Odin.

WORLD TREE

Known as Yggdrasil, this immense ash tree connects the nine worlds of Norse mythology. Dragons, eagles, and stags are said to live in its branches.

The adventure continues . . .

Join Alva as she solves her next mystery, this time taking to the sea aboard a viking longship! Can she navigate through stormy waters to reach her destination, and will she find herself any closer to discovering the whereabouts of her father?

Janina Ramirez is a medievalist, cultural historian, and broadcaster who specializes in decoding symbols and uncovering the bigger picture behind works of art and literature.

She is course director for the Undergraduate Certificate and Diploma in History of Art at Oxford University, and has been writing and presenting history programmes for BBC television and radio since 2010. She has a weekly podcast, 'The Art Detective', produced by History Hit. She has also written a number of academic books and articles on the early medieval period.

She lives in Oxfordshire with her husband, son, daughter, and three cats. When she gets a quiet moment (rarely!) she likes to listen to audiobooks, paint and go on historical adventures.

Here are some other stories we think you'll love...

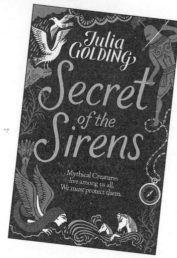